P.P. Fourie

The Heart Is the Size of a Fist

KWELA BOOKS

Kwela Books,
an imprint of NB Publishers,
a division of Media24 Boeke (Pty) Ltd
40 Heerengracht, Cape Town, South Africa
PO Box 879, Cape Town, South Africa, 8000
www.kwela.com

Cover design by Michiel Botha
Typography by Susan Bloemhof
Set in 12 on 18pt Ehrhard

Printed by **novus print**, a division of Novus Holdings

First edition, first impression 2021

ISBN: 978-0-7957-0998-2
ISBN: 978-0-7957-0999-9 (epub)

For my mother.

'Anything processed by memory is fiction.'

– David Shields

'We live with such easy assumptions, don't we? For instance, that memory equals events plus time. But it's all much odder than this. Who was it said that memory is what we thought we'd forgotten? And it ought to be obvious to us that time doesn't act as a fixative, rather as a solvent. But it's not convenient – it's not useful – to believe this; it doesn't help us get on with our lives; so we ignore it.'

– Julian Barnes, *The Sense of an Ending*

'Memory's truth, because memory has its own special kind. It selects, eliminates, alters, exaggerates, minimizes, glorifies, and vilifies also; but in the end it creates its own reality, its heterogeneous but usually coherent version of events; and no sane human being ever trusts someone else's version more than his own.'

– Salman Rushdie, *Midnight's Children*

TESSERAE

TIME PAST

TIME PRESENT

TIME PAST

I REMEMBER,

in no particular order:

– The binary star system Capella, which orbits itself, a duet, like lovers.

– A couple in embrace, beholding in wonder the end of the world, tinted all honey and blood.

– A boy wearing make-up, timing an oncoming car as he runs to cross a road on a hot, hot day.

– A lover, drowsy and naked, assuring me that something beautiful, something gentle will remain, even if we become monsters.

– Snow falling on water, dissolving on the surface of a lake.

– A woman, bereft and in agony, enjoining me to choose pain over safety.

– The rushing sadness associated with profound feeling, awe.

– Always, always: him, her.

– The music, the words,

$\qquad$ the splendid imperfections.

TONES OF GLASS

Music. Carole King. 'Tapestry'. Vodka and tomato juice. I hear my mother's laughter from the kitchen, from the lounge, elsewhere in the house, but I can tell she does not mean it. She is not laughing at all. She is taking care of the other guests.

I am seven years old, very nearly eight. I have my face flat against a parquet floor, tracing the outline of the wooden blocks with a fingernail. I am listening, too. I do not wish to look up and see. But I can hear, I listen.

The worst thing about the evening is their disregard. They are indifferent to me. He and she pretend that they are by themselves. My being, and my being there (not far from the two of them), is of no consequence. They are talking between themselves, soft fricatives, gentle plosives, things said and unsaid, looks, glances. I do not exist.

Whatever it is that I am, I am not my father's son. Not tonight. Not now. This is vaguely distressing. I am aware that I am witness – no, party – to something transgressive. This is also vaguely thrilling.

There are twelve narrow ribbings around the metal cap. Again and again I count them; an odd satisfaction. Something significant is happening. Everything will be different now. To this day I will not drink tomato juice.

She wears Cameo pantihose.

I recognise this from the two butterflies embroidered on her ankles. In the television advertisement there is a line about this: 'Cameo, let your legs do the talking.'

She is not wearing any shoes. From where I am, I can see her feet, her toes inside the pantihose, without needing to adjust the position of my head. She touches the floor with her toes, then she lifts her feet, then she repeats the action. Her feet are forever moving. Touch, lift. Touch, lift. Touch, lift.

I recognise something familiar but also unusual in this moment, in this place. Something between her and my father. I am not upset; maybe only curious. Perhaps, with the two of them, I am worried that my mother will open the door.

I will myself completely invisible. Dim. Dimmer. Gone.

My father flirts with Vivienne; Vivienne flirts with my father.

I imagine myself as a frond, curled from within the fern in the corner, or as one of the dead insects stuck in the spider's web beneath. I am flat on my stomach. I am become the floor, and I am cold.

'I do love you, you know.'

(My father always speaks English if he does not want me to understand.)

'Oh yes?'

She smiles and opens her legs a bit wider. The fabric around her legs slides from side to side, makes little clicking shooting sounds against her stockings. Somewhere way above is her face; a thin line of white and pink, out of focus: her teeth, her tongue.

'We can leave,' he says, lifting the glass from the wooden side table. I imagine a ring of moisture on the wood. 'Elope like youngsters,' he explains. I consider fetching something, a rag or a dishcloth, to wipe down the wood. That glass belongs on a coaster. But I do not move; I know better.

Vivienne now looks at me. I can tell that she is excited. I feel her look. I am trying to remove the dark strip of dirt from under my fingernail, with a toothpick. She knows I am here. I am here. I think she likes this.

She says my father's name. 'Don't be silly, you have a nice life here.' She is still watching me; I will not look at her. 'Try to think of me as your . . . an intimate availability. A presence you can touch without obligation.'

'And I thought you only wanted to fuck.'

Both of them laugh, draw in breaths.

I can't dislodge the dirt from under my nail. I keep on digging with the toothpick. It is starting to hurt now. I do not care. I do not care. I do not care.

He picks up his drink again; keeping his eyes on her, he empties the glass with a long, slow swallow. The ice makes a pleasant sound. They laugh once more, a bit too loudly, and she says something to him that I do not understand.

'Paul, please fetch Daddy another tomato juice,' he says in Afrikaans. They both turn to look at me, smiling.

I arrange my face into a smile. Get up. Yawn. I skip out of the room, towards the kitchen. I feel triumphant. I do not know why.

* * *

It is later that same evening. The guests are leaving and my father is saying goodbye to Vivienne. He leans against her green Mini Cooper as they share a cigarette.

I will do it now.

I find my mother in the lounge. She is in a chair, a large black plastic bag next to her. She must have been cleaning up, throwing away serviettes, emptying the ashtrays, and then she must have sat down. From where I stand it looks as though she is waiting for something; she is staring out the window, into the darkness. I sense she is thinking of something else, somewhere different, and it takes a few seconds for her to become aware that I am in the room. Then, when she notices, she smiles.

'Hey you. Still awake?'

Suddenly I feel very sad and I get onto her lap. I want to cry. Now I will do it. Car doors outside, conversations far away. I push the front of my face into her neck, in amongst the auburn hair near her ear, and I wait, I draw in breath.

I whisper as softly as possible.

'There's something I want to tell Mommy.'

I try to move closer to her ear. I need to say this without hearing it myself.

I smell shampoo. I close my eyes.

'I want to tell you what Daddy and Tannie Vivienne spoke about.'

I report the conversation, word for word, in English.

* * *

Later, after the raised voices, after my father has stormed out into the night, to *her*, I hear my mother get up from her chair, hear her walk towards my room. I pretend to be asleep. In the dark, she strokes my head and sits on the side of the bed for a long time; then she gets up and walks to the toilet. I hear her throw up. I imagine avocado dip and tomato juice.

* * *

I am eight years old. Early December 1980. The Eastern Cape. We are renting a small farm near Oyster Bay, for the holidays. There is a vegetable garden. We do not know it, but this is our last summer holiday together as a family. Earlier in the day, we had lunch with Athol Fugard and his wife. I played with tortoises on a lawn while the men – one young, one old – visited together on the wraparound stoep.

My father is on a high for the rest of the day. When he is happy, we are all happy. That night after dinner my father dances with my mother. I watch them in wonder. This is rare. This is heaven. Yes, there is wine, and I am nervous, always nervous. But all is well.

The next morning we go to a small supermarket near the ocean. The newspaper headline says: 'John Lennon shot dead by fan.' This means nothing to me. Silently, my father dumps the groceries in the back of the car, starts the car but starts to weep. My mother has to drive. We are all very, very quiet. Later, my father disappears from the house and returns with bottles. Green bottles and see-through bottles. I go to my room, then outside. Listen to the tones of glass. This music I know.

Later still, the light sinking to evening, my father instructs me to bring out the small model plane that we have recently finished build-ing. My mother murmurs that the wind is perhaps quite strong. My father ignores her. He stands on a hill, next to a small wood, and launches the little plane into the air. The plane is lifted instantly, glid-ing high, high, higher, then suddenly it veers on the wind and comes down hard, into the trees. I whimper. He tells me to shut up. We never see the plane again.

He insists on making dinner. Beef stew. Except instead of potatoes he uses green apples. It tastes awful. I tell him it is delicious, and he keeps on dishing it into our plates. There will be hell if we do not eat. There will be hell anyway. This is hell.

Late that night he announces that we will leave Oyster Bay early the next morning. He has decided that we are going home. I plead with him. He mocks me. '*Please*, Daddy; *please*, Daddy; *please*, Daddy,' he says.

I go out into the wind. I beg God to kill him.

* * *

I am twelve years old. December 1984. The three of us are having a braai on the Swartberg mountain pass. The view is spectacular. You can see all the way to the future, to heaven. My parents are divorced, but my father is staying with us for a few weeks. He is clean, he is dry, he has joined Alcoholics Anonymous. He makes us feel better than anything in the world.

He and I are running down the dirt road towards the car. The excited dogs run alongside. My mother is taking photographs of us, from a distance. We recently saw *Gallipoli* together, and we shout out the lines from the movie as we run:

My father: What are your legs?

Me: Springs. Steel springs.

My father: What are they going to do?

Me: Hurl me down the track.

My father: How fast can you run?

Me: As fast as a leopard.

My father: How fast are you going to run?

Me: As fast as a leopard!

My father: Then let's see you do it!

I laugh, he laughs, she laughs, and we collapse around the braai area, on the grass, panting for breath. I feel like a god.

* * *

I am twenty years old. I am taking a weekend break from university, visiting my father. My father and his wife, and their son, my half-brother, who is nearly four years old. My grandmother was also visiting, and has just left.

My father and I are still awake. He has been drinking steadily since his mother left, and I am crafting excuses to leave. My grandmother. I should have known; she brings out the worst in everyone. A Dementor, a snake, she has sucked the joy out of all of us, and my father is filling the void in the only way he knows.

She has left my father a gift. A large painting by a famous South African artist, oil on canvas, approximately one metre by one metre; ornate gilt frame. Objectively, the work is stunning. Skilfully executed. Deftly proportioned. A rendering of the crucifixion from the perspective of the crucified. The result is a dramatically elevated vantage point, Christ witnessing the witnesses, eye contact riveted. Here, Roman soldiers for crowd control; there, a mob. Angry, anxious, curious. Familiar characters too: a mother bereft, eyes wild; weeping women trying to comfort her. To the side, a small group of petrified men. Dark colours, a strange sky, emotive.

But our own perspective is clouded by the painting's provenance, my grandmother its most recent owner. She had emphasised the painting's monetary value: officially appraised at over fifty thousand rand.

Now it is late, near midnight, and I am reading on a deck chair, on the front stoep. My father and his new family live on a vast plot of land in Penhill, where people keep horses and dogs and scarce company. Neighbours are few and far between. It has been raining softly since the sinking afternoon. I love this weather. My father joins me.

He is drunk, but not violent, yet I know how quickly this can change, so I anticipate his arrows, ready to block. I am friendly and acquiescent, but I commit to nothing. My demeanour is more reticent than my roiling inner life. This narrative, this role: I am quite the expert.

My father has hauled the painting onto the stoep. He places it carefully against a chair and we study it together. He says something about Saint Augustine, then segues into a lecture about visual perspective and the medieval gaze. Now he is talking about Marxism and the commodification of art. I encourage him, I nod, I am dutiful and intelligent.

My father opens a tin of solvent. He takes a brush and delicately applies the pungent, transparent liquid to the painting. This will dissolve the protective layer and loosen the oil, he explains. I am transfixed, my eyes gleaming like a child's as he witnesses a house on fire. When my father has completed the task, he tells me that this process does not damage the painting; at this point one could just wait for the solvent to dissolve, then apply a fixative, and the painting would be safe.

He gets up. Lifts the painting and holds it in front of him. Walks out from under the roofed stoep and away from the house. Places the painting on a wooden chair, solitary on the lawn, turns it to face me, about ten metres away. My father asks if I can see the image clearly. I nod. Then he joins me back on the veranda, and we share a cigarette.

We watch as a gentle rain washes the suffering Christ into a dull, uniform grey.

* * *

A Tuesday afternoon in September. I am thirty-three years old. Soon it will be my birthday.

My lover is fellating me, both of us fully dressed. In the moment,

I know that our relationship is over, and it occurs to me that I am, right now, the age that Jesus was when He died. I must have thought aloud, because my lover pauses, speaks, but I cannot make out what he is saying. I coax his head down, reminding him that it is impolite to speak when one's mouth is full. He winks, and continues.

Near the brink, I stare at the light above us. The dead moths caught inside the glass fitting. I turn my head sideways, and I close my eyes and I am flying like a plane, light, weightless. I am made of balsawood. I am running down a mountain, ecstatic. I feel an image dissolve before my eyes.

I will end the relationship. Later that day. It is the right thing to do. But now I feel sorry for him, and so I place my hand on his head and push my fingers deep into his hair. That lovely hair. On that lovely head. I will miss him.

THE LATE

Not long ago, at the end of one season and the start of another, I am reading a book review somewhere online when my father's name comes up, in the footnotes. *The late _____.*

The late.

I have seen almost nothing of my father since Friday 18 February 1994. He has been absent for most of my adult life – and in truth for most of my life before that. Over the past quarter century I first feigned and then stopped needing to feign indifference to him. And yet, there it is:

The late _____.

My father achieved minor celebrity in the 1970s as a playwright, peaked, and then withered. But this novelty – death – intrigues me. I e-mail the author of the book review and ask him when my father died. The man responds within hours, saying that he was recalling sources from the late 1990s who indicated that my father had committed suicide.

Appropriate, I think.

The author promises to check again.

A day or so later I learn that my father is still alive.

I lose interest again. Or rather, I marvel anew at my father's ability not to kill himself after all, being who he is – or was.

This is just after Mother's Day, and then Father's Day follows a few weeks later. In my family we never celebrate these days; they are silly commercial schemes. The furthest I would go was some years back, to thank my mother on Father's Day, for being a 'double parent'. (I thought that was very clever.)

This puts me in the mood to reconsider my mother. Two memories come to mind.

* * *

In the winter of 1982 (my tenth birthday is a few months later) my father follows us to Oudtshoorn, to where we had fled from Bloemfontein after my mother finally left him. He mixes alcohol and pills. There is a nasty scene, violence – the usual. But since we had left him some months earlier he had acquired a .38 Special revolver. Two shots are fired – one goes into the stove and the other goes into a kitchen shelf. We lock the front door behind us, and run into the night – my mother, our ageing Rottweiler Bruni, and me.

It is very cold. We find refuge on the outside stairs at the side of an empty house a bit further down the road. We can still hear him scream and shout, but he does not leave the house to come after us. And there we sit the whole night, waiting for light, waiting for him to pass out. My mother has to teach music the next day, and I have midyear exams. Winter in the Little Karoo is harsh (there is snow on the Swartberg mountains), but I have this blazing memory, this glorious image, when I think about that night: my mother sitting bare-armed and straight, with her back to me. She has taken off her jersey and given it to me, to sleep on. In front of me (between my mother and me) lies Bruni, keeping me warm. And in front of the dog sits my mother, guarding a nine-year-old boy, and guarding a Rottweiler.

* * *

My second memory is from May 1997. We are in Paris, where I had gone on a scholarship, and my mother is visiting me on what is her first trip outside of South Africa. We will start a backpacking tour of Europe the next day (one of those hop-on-hop-off bus affairs, lasting a month). My mother has brought her facial wax, and wants to get rid of the small growth of hair on her upper lip. We are both smokers back then, so we have something with which to light a fire, but in my reconfigured *chambre de bonne*, on the sixth floor, no stove or heating appliance is allowed. There is nothing we can use to melt the wax. What to do?

I live on the rue des Écoles, which is two blocks from the Notre Dame cathedral. After a brief conference, I walk down the six flights of stairs, out the front door, and down to the cathedral. I take out a ten franc piece, and buy a single votive candle, glance guiltily and un-catholicly at Jesus, and walk back out the front door of the cathedral, past the spot where history tells us a medieval queen (I forget which one) was assassinated.

Back in my room, my mother uses the votive candle to heat her facial wax, and we laugh, and smoke cigarettes, and drink brandy neat from paper cups.

THE NIGHT OF THE GUN

My father is quite high by the time he discovers that his revolver is missing. He is furious, in a rage. I have hidden it, along with the car keys; I understand that opiates and firearms together portend ominous things. My father hits me across my back, striking me down, and instructs me to fetch it this instant, or I'll be sorry. I know that my mother faces either vicious physical attack – inevitably, imminently – if I do not collect the weapon, or possible death, by shooting, if I fetch it. As I walk with the heavy thing in my hand, from the outbuilding back to the house, to give it to my father, I try to cock the hammer, so that I can shoot and kill him, but my hands are too small. I know I will not be able to pull the trigger without cocking the hammer, and in any case, I will not be able to shoot it straight, from the effort of holding it, and from the shaking. I cry quietly, in frustration and in despair, because, although I have the resolve and understand the simple utility of it, I lack the physical strength to kill my father.

A SENTIMENTAL EDUCATION

In Gustave Flaubert's novel *L'Éducation sentimentale* there is a section right at the end of the penultimate chapter that I find deeply affecting. I vividly remember the first time I read it – and had it read to me, in beautiful, sonorous French – in a windowless lecture room in what must have been my second or possibly my third year at university.

If one is fortunate, one experiences a handful of formative, educational moments that are truly memorable. Or rather, they are moments that turn out to be truly educational and formative, that have a multiplier effect on the life of the mind. To me such moments are closely associated with great beauty, interiority; they confirm that one is not alone, and that one may just, after all, be able to express that occasional mysterious instance when what is authentic meets what is universal.

I respond physically when I encounter such moments in art. I inhale quickly but quietly, or for a few seconds I stop breathing altogether. Often, I want to laugh or cry, and if I experience this in the company of others I look about me slyly, slowly, to see if they too notice what I have noticed, feel what I have felt, and are delighted. I am able to recall a few such works of art, and the instances I first experienced them:

– Hermann Hesse's novel *Demian*, when I was sixteen.

– *Bagdad Cafe* at the Cinema Acropolis, in Oudtshoorn, later that same year.

– Bach's 'Wachet auf, ruft uns die Stimme', played on a church organ by my mother when I was fifteen.

– Brahms' *Ein deutsches Requiem*, second movement, when the choir joins the percussion, when I was twenty.

– A painting scandalously depicting the crucifixion from the perspective of the person on the cross, in the State Hermitage Museum in Saint Petersburg, in January 2006.

– Ravel's Piano Concerto in G Major, live at the Sydney Opera House, in November 2009.

– Whirling dervishes, in a caravanserai in Cappadocia, on a warm evening in September 2005.

– And the most enduring, the most special of them all: Arvo Pärt's 'Cantus in Memoriam Benjamin Britten', when I was not quite twenty years old.

At the end of that chapter in Flaubert's novel, Frédéric (the protagonist) meets with the love of his life, Madame Arnoux, one last time. She is older than he, and they are unable ever to align their lives, and be together. It is tragic. In the final scene, they talk together for a bit, and just before she departs she removes her comb and cuts off a strand of her hair, leaving it as a parting gift. She then leaves the room without fuss or ceremony, walks down the stairs, and gets into a carriage that takes her away. Frédéric watches her departure from the upstairs window, and the chapter ends with one final line, four words: '*Et ce fut tout.*' And that was all.

When I lived in my tiny Parisian room just below the roof of 41, rue des Écoles, I often stood on my balcony and regarded the street six floors below, recalling that scene. There was no Madame Arnoux, and no Frédéric, but there was still much to see and experience. Every day at 4 a.m. I woke from the sound of metal shutters being opened, at the laundromat on the ground floor right across the road. This was followed by the sound of glass bottles being emptied from a large waste container, in the side street next to the shop below.

Later, around 9 a.m. every day, there was a tiny, ancient Asian woman in the apartment slightly below mine, across the road, doing stretches and then performing what looked like some kind of prayer ritual. She repeated this in the late afternoon, when the sun shone on her and on the plants and the carpet around her. There may have been a shrine of some sort outside my line of vision, as she always spoke to herself and bowed in the same direction.

Elsewhere in the building across from mine I had sight of an artist, doing something on large pieces of blank paper or canvas that he kept on an easel. The artist worked facing my direction, which was intriguing to watch, but it meant that I could never see what he was creating. If these people ever noticed me, I do not know. They probably did, but they were better at the subtle social protocols of not noticing or acknowledging neighbours across the road. Whatever the case may be, I certainly remember them, and there is something important in just that, as though life was telling me to pay attention, that this is my life, and that this – all of this – matters.

Three other people I remember, from around this time.

A woman in an underground transit area, in the Métro system. Rush hour. People everywhere, in a hurry. She is maybe forty years old. She seems to be in agony – not physical, but something existential. She walks very slowly. Her face looks like it belongs on Michelangelo's *Pietà*. Time does not apply to her. I use the same route at the same time of the day, three times in the following week, to look for her. I never see her again.

A German exchange student in my research methodology class. He reminds me that it has been three years since the end of apartheid. He asks me if I am ashamed. He says that I should be. I say to his friend that it is amusing to be taught a lesson in shame and moral outrage by a German, in the late twentieth century. We never speak again.

On Thursdays after class I walk back to my building, using side streets that take me towards and then through the Luxembourg Gardens. I sit on a bench and read my book. I become aware of another person close by, also reading. It is one of the young men working in the garden, preparing a flower bed nearby. He is on his break. He is reading Baudelaire's *Les Fleurs du mal*. The flowers of evil.

In February 1997, my neighbour Edward and I decide to escape Valentine's Day in Paris, and take the fast train to Amsterdam, for a weekend. He is keen to use some soft drugs, and I have never been to the Netherlands. Edward comes from a wealthy family and is biding his time in Paris faking a Master's degree exchange while he waits for his girlfriend to join him in the summer. Edward spends his days revelling in indolence, reading novels. *Gormenghast. A Tale of Two Cities. A Moveable Feast.* From the latter, he reads me a quote:

'If you are lucky enough to have lived in Paris as a young man, then wherever you go for the rest of your life, it stays with you, for Paris is a moveable feast.'

Edward thinks this is hysterically funny, and trite. He affects that boredom of the affluent. He has poor social skills; I feel sorry for Edward. He knows a Serb called Zoran, who lives in central Amsterdam and with whom we can stay. Edward warns me that Zoran is a homosexual, but generally friendly. He just thinks I should know. I nod.

While Edward is reading more of the Hemingway, I am determined to take in as much as I can, through the carriage window. Even at bullet train speed, there is much to observe. The landscape, the changes as France becomes Belgium, and later when Belgium becomes Holland. The sky seems remarkably low. At one point, we become peckish and I fetch us some coffees. After I drink mine I remain standing, and Edward jokingly suggests that I do a little dance, so I try to tap dance for about ten seconds. Edward seems embarrassed.

The night before our journey I went out with the neighbour who lived in the room on my other side, a Macedonian called Sašo. Edward's comment about Zoran's homosexuality reminds me of him. Sašo was studying Engineering at the École Normale Supérieure, and did not want to return to Skopje; it was clear that the Balkans were falling apart. Sašo took me to a nightclub in the Marais, right on the other side of the Notre Dame cathedral, not too far from where we lived. He danced with other men, as I sat entranced, sipping cider from a bowl.

When we arrive in Amsterdam, Edward takes me to a pub and we have a *witbier*, and some *kroketten*. We walk and walk the canals and the side streets while we wait for Zoran to get home, at an appointed time. Amsterdam is exotic: small, beautiful, colourful, seedy. Much less grand than Paris, but more liveable. The idea of soft drugs does not excite me, so I do not share Edward's eager inspection of the various cafés and menus. In the end Edward decides that he will find something the next day, and we go for a walk in the red-light district instead. Prostitutes regard us with boredom from behind glass on their high stools, semi-naked, as tourists gawk and whoop in the narrow streets.

By the time we arrive at Zoran's apartment, we are famished. Edward reminds me again about the gay thing, and I promise him that I will not forget, and that I will be civil. Zoran is polite and friendly. He gives us thin soup, something citrus and cucumber, 'just to refresh', and then he prepares a fine meal consisting of lots of cream, cheese, and something meaty. It is delicious, and he watches us eat it with satisfaction. He is in his mid-thirties, and has been living in Amsterdam for five years. He fled Belgrade as soon as the war broke out, as the government was forcing all able-bodied men into the army.

After dinner Zoran asks us if we want to watch some porn. Edward declines instantly, asks for another beer instead. I am fine with the linden berry extract, thank you. Would we like some drugs? I have a sense of dread, but Edward is keen. Zoran rummages through a metal container and emerges with two mysterious tablets.

'What is this?' he asks himself. 'Oh yes, now I remember. Nice.' He laughs conspiratorially. Edward and I decline the offer.

In the end Zoran finds Edward some weed to smoke, after which Edward promptly vomits and goes to sleep. 'Oops,' says Zoran.

He turns to me. 'And now, what about you, sir?' Zoran asks, not unkindly.

'Tell me about the war,' I say. 'How did you get out?'

'Ah, the war,' says Zoran, in a heavy Serbian accent, lighting another cigarette. 'What is there to say about the fucking war.' He seems sad.

We talk into the night, with Edward snoring on a mattress in another part of the single-room apartment. The only thing that happens between Zoran and me is that we become quite good friends. We drink a lot of linden berry extract, and at one point he becomes tearful when he tells me about the pet dogs he had to leave behind in Serbia.

Life, it was becoming clear to me, demands constant aesthetic and moral awareness, choice, and consequence. There is profundity in the mundane. My life is happening. Pay attention. It is all part of a ceaseless sentimental education. *Et ce fut tout.*

HESTER AGNES AND THE BLUE TEACUP

On the morning of her death, my mother's mother – Hester Agnes – asks for honey with her tea. This is unusual. Hester is a diabetic, requiring injections twice a day, and so my mother turns and looks at her with disapproval. From her bed my grandmother winks at her daughter, smiles, and asks my mother to bring the cat (and a pillow) on her way back from the kitchen. Hester has been feeling poorly for a day or two; staying in bed is out of the ordinary, and concerning. Although she is only fifty-six years old, there is a history of a weak heart, and recently there has been oedema.

But my mother does not want to spoil the mood with petty prescription, and so she just shakes her head and, sighing parentally, dramatically, she turns to fetch the tea from the kitchen.

'When I come back I'll tell you about my news,' she says.

'Don't forget the cat,' says Hester as her daughter leaves the room.

When my mother returns, Hester is sitting up, still under the covers, but with her back against the headboard.

'Thank you,' she says as my mother passes her the blue cup in a white saucer.

'One teaspoon only,' my mother says, and Hester sips the tea, closes her eyes, and smiles, enjoying the taste of the honey.

'Thank you,' she says again, looking about the room. 'And Vaaltyn?'

she asks – meaning the cat. My mother ignores her, sits down beside her on the bed and puts her hands on her legs in front of her, looking at Hester like someone with a secret.

'So I think I'm pregnant,' says my mother, *sotto voce*. She blinks, smiling defiantly, desperately. Hester pauses, puts the cup in its saucer, and turns her head to face her daughter directly.

'How long?'

'Five weeks,' says my mother.

'That's not so very long,' says my grandmother, taking her daughter's hand.

'I know,' says my mother, 'but it's longer than previous times.'

'The doctors told you not to hope,' says my grandmother, gently. Hester can see that this is not the best comment, at just that moment, and says immediately, 'Ah, but wouldn't it be wonderful?' My mother beams.

'Have you told him?' asks Hester.

My mother shakes her head no. 'I'll tell him tonight, when he gets back. He wants a girl, but I know it's a boy,' says my mother. 'Actually, I just want a healthy baby,' my mother qualifies.

'A healthy baby, yes,' says Hester. My mother looks at her, recalling her mother's own loss of babies. Four times she carried boys to term, but three times the infants only survived for a few months. The fourth boy – Hennie – lived to the age of four, a healthy, happy child. Then, on a dark day, they discovered bruises on his body. The next day there were more, and he died within two weeks, taken by leukaemia.

Involuntarily my mother turns her eyes slightly to look at the blue teacup in the white saucer, next to Hester on the side table. Her mother sees her look, smiles, and looks out the window.

A month before Hennie became ill, Hester had washed all her crockery and put it out in the sun, as she did every other weekend.

From inside the house she heard a smash, a child's delighted laugh, and then more smashes. Four-year-old Hennie was smashing the individual pieces of crockery against the back garden wall. When he saw his mother he laughed, pointing at the shards gathered on the ground, giggling, ecstatic. Hester told my mother that this was her most special memory of Hennie; she passed him piece after piece – plates, saucers, cups – and delighted in the joy that followed every smash. Of everything there, only the blue teacup remained, and ever since Hennie's death this is what she used to have her first cup of tea in the morning.

'A healthy baby, yes,' my mother says again. My grandmother seems to remember where she is, looks back at her daughter.

'I think I'm leaving this world, my darling,' she says. My mother is silent for a second, then puts the back of her hand on Hester's forehead. It is damp.

'Don't make false promises,' says my mother, but she is worried. Hester laughs at this comment, and as my mother gets up, to phone the doctor, Hester says there's no rush, and asks my mother to stay with her.

By the time the doctor arrives my grandmother is dead. My mother sat with her until the end, and closed her eyes when it was over. Hester looks now as if she is asleep, with her head on her hand, against the pillow. The breeze from the window plays with Hester's hair, and the movement creates a trompe l'oeil, the semblance of life.

My mother gets up and takes the blue teacup in the white saucer, leaving the room with the doctor. At the door she turns around to look at her mother. The cat is asleep on Hester's feet.

'Do you want me to bring out the cat?' asks the doctor.

'No,' says my mother. 'Just let them sleep for a bit.'

THE TORTOISE

I am born on a Tuesday in the spring, around five in the afternoon, shortly after a shower of rain. The sun has come out again, the light more ochre than clear, with petrichor abundant.

My mother is admitted to hospital three months before her due date, because her organs are failing. My father is asked whom they should save, if the choice needs to be made.

'The mother,' he says. I approve of this, when I learn of it later on.

When the Caesarean is required, five weeks early, my father rushes to the hospital, but has to stop his car for a small tortoise crossing the road, counterintuitively, in the city. He picks up the tortoise and puts it in a brown paper bag.

Once everyone is known to be safe, baby sleeping, mother emerging from anaesthesia, my father presents the tortoise as a gift to the new-born, and to the room. There are quiet smiles. The new parents hold hands, speak softly to each other, and watch their son breathe in a nearby cot, as the tortoise slowly inspects the room.

WHERE THE WORLD ENDS

When I am four years old I become quite ill. I am a healthy child, so this is unusual and kind of exotic. I remember a few visits to the doctor; there is also a vague, feverish spell during which I am later told I sleepwalk and suffer febrile seizures.

My illness keeps me at home, unable to go to the playschool where I go in the daytime while my mother works. This is during a period when my parents are not married; they divorced when I was two years old, and remarried a few months before I turned five. I cannot remember a nanny of any kind looking after me during this time, so my mother must have taken some time off from work.

I remember being by myself for long stretches of time; solitude is my most prominent impression of this period. Not that this was a problem: as an only child I was used to being by myself, and as my parents moved around quite a bit during my first decade of life, I had no close friends. This does not mean that I was lonely – on the contrary, I was so used to being by myself that this was the norm, and in truth I cannot remember ever feeling lonely as a child.

I remember this period of illness and convalescence as a peaceful, happy time. I follow the progress of what I now think must be a winter sun on the carpet in the living room, moving along as spots of sunlight make their way across the room. There are vinyl records of children's stories that I sometimes listen to, and I also have access to my parents' music collection. There are some children's books that I page through, to study the images, although I am not much of a reader. Instead of playing with toys, I amuse myself by using empty upturned ashtrays as spaceships, and the patterns on the carpet become roads for my small assortment of little vehicles. I most enjoy playing with a collection of small, round magnets that are painted different colours: the invisible push and pull – through cloth, glass, paper – is fascinating, like magic made real.

My father's visits are unusual events, as he now lives in a different city. When he does visit, I have even more time to myself, although the three of us do sometimes go out to dinner. Fancy places: I remember dinner jackets and crisp white cloth serviettes, waiters pulling out chairs, ready with lighters for my parents' cigarettes. I now realise that this must have been a period of reconciliation for them.

Late in my recovery my father arrives on a Friday evening on a motorcycle, for a weekend. I remember feeling embarrassed about not recognising him in his helmet. He sports a new moustache. We are friendly, polite, and a little shy with each other. We have dinner at home, as I am not quite well enough to go out, with other people around, and I remember soup (yes, it must be winter) on which my mother drifts pieces of toast cut into triangles, so that they look like yachts on the ocean. My mother praises me to my father, saying that I have been such a good boy during the past few weeks.

My father wakes me up very early the next morning. It is still night, as there is no hint of dawn visible through my window. My father is friendly and conspiratorial. I am to hurry, as the three of us are about to embark on a small adventure, something really special. My father explains that he is going to take my mother and me somewhere, to show us where the world ends. This is the most mysterious thing I have ever heard of, and I enjoy the sense of urgent theatre that accompanies us as we hurry quietly down the outside staircase of the block of flats towards my mother's car.

It is apparent that my parents have been planning this adventure for a while, as I share the backseat (heavy blanket, pillows) with various containers of food, snacks, and a thermos of coffee. It is cold, but we are all warmed by the energy of the moment, my father playing coy, serious, and vague when I interrogate him about the purpose of our journey. I will have to wait and see. Where the world ends – this sounds dangerous and thrilling. We drive for what feels like hours, well out of the city and into the night, listening to Carole King and Frida Boccara on the tape deck. I fall asleep.

When they wake me up it is almost completely quiet. There is the odd shriek of birds, somewhere far above our heads, but I cannot make them out. It is still quite dark, with no houses or any other kinds of lights visible at all. We are parked on the side of a road, and there is no traffic. The wind is freezing, though not very strong. My mother picks me up and tells me that it is almost time, that my father will reveal his secret – where the world ends – any second now. From the ambient light it is clear that dawn is imminent; the birds are getting excited. Somewhere behind me my father is humming the chorus from something that we listened to in the car; he is unpacking what from the corner of my eye looks like a small table and chairs.

'Here it comes,' he says. 'Get ready.'

My mother nods at my father and he takes me from her, turning me around to witness the most amazing sight I have ever seen in my life. Where the world ends. The sun is just appearing on the horizon. The red, orange, yellow and white glows are spectacular and warm, blinding me. As my eyes adjust I become aware of a landscape transformed. No, the actual land has disappeared completely. The edge of the road where we are parked gives way to an endless abyss, as though a giant has taken some monstrous instrument and hacked the planet away, straight down from where we are. There at the bottom, and then stretching out all the way across to the horizon, is an ocean bathed in red and yellow. The earth is gone, and it is the most beautiful thing I have ever seen.

'Dawn. Honey and blood.' It is my father's voice. I turn to look at him, and to look at my mother. I am sitting on his arm and his other arm is around her. They are shining, as though the light is not coming from the dawn sun, but emerging from the two of them. They are smiling, looking not at me, but taking in the wonder playing out in front of us.

They have brought me all the way from the city to the top of the wall of the Hartbeespoort Dam. We are parked on the wall, right at the top, and we are facing east. There are no other cars, and for one landlocked boy this is the closest he has ever come to where the world ends.

After a while, as the sun delinks from the horizon and starts to lift, above the planet, we sit down at our little table and share a meal consisting of devilled eggs, sausages, soft white sandwiches, and coffee. We laugh into our visible breaths, we are relaxed and enjoy each other.

Later on I become sleepy and my mother tucks me in under the blanket and on the pillows on the backseat of the car. I fall asleep watching them talking quietly, holding each other, smiling, suspended above the place where the world ends.

THE HAPPY PRINCE

When I am six years old we live in Clarens, in a vast old sandstone house with a high ceiling on the edge of the village, next to a little forest that leads into the mountains. By now we have been living in the Eastern Free State for about eighteen months, since right after my parents remarried. My mother works as a music teacher at a secondary school in Bethlehem, about half an hour's drive away, and my father is writing full-time.

A few years ago his play *The Plot* was produced by the Performing Arts Council of the Transvaal. The play was a critical and a commercial success, and there are hopes that he will produce something comparable soon. There is a sense of expectation, a sense of promise, that the gods are smiling on him, and on us.

I associate the smell of pipe tobacco and old books with my father's study, where I often busy myself on the wooden floor while he works. When he is not writing, he makes charcoal sketches of famous authors' faces on large pieces of butcher paper. He is also drinking. Not so much that there is a sense of siege, of horror – that comes later. At this stage he just sleeps a lot.

I do not remember having great affection for my father at this time. Not disaffection or fear either, mind you. He is simply an unknown entity. To me his physical presence is always temporary. He has been

41

absent for some years, until fairly recently, and father-son activities such as kicking a ball around or flying a kite are rare events. Mostly such activities feel forced, or staged, somewhat ridiculous. They do not come naturally to him, and they do not come naturally to me. We both feel most at ease just being in each other's company, father–son in the abstract, sharing a space but busy with our own projects, and respectively, respectfully discrete.

One day I ask him how long it will be until my mother gets home from work. He shows me the hands of an alarm clock and tells me that she will arrive when the short hand is 'here' and the long hand is 'there'. I look at this little machine that has such power to determine our physical whereabouts, and ask my father whether we cannot just move the hands of the clock to those positions, so that my mother can appear? This seems logical to me, but I am told that this is not how it works, and that the clock needs to be left alone to move at its own pace. I now understand something about the nature of time, and waiting.

A few years ago, as an adult, I went back to Clarens – by now a twee, self-consciously arty little town. I headed to my forest first – an abundance of tall trees a little way into the mountains from where we lived all those years ago. I recalled myself as a small boy, alone in the woods after the rain. It was very still, very quiet, and I smelled the pines and the rain, and I heard something, something friendly, maybe a bird, and down the hill, in dappled light, the rivulet trickled, and the entire forest was mine: the prince of trees.

I walked around the old schoolyard, which was empty during the summer holiday. The school itself is small, consisting of two sandstone buildings. I looked through the window and saw tiny desks and blackboards near the floor. I was embarrassed when a well-dressed older woman gave a little cough behind me, and asked if she could be of assistance. She was the principal, though of course not from when I went to school there. I apologised for snooping around, but when I told her that I had gone to this school, she invited me to her office at the back, and she dug out the old pupil enrolment log. And there was my name, our address, and my parents' daytime contact details, written in my father's idiosyncratic, clear handwriting. He had used his own pen, the same green ink. Odd feeling. I remember that first school day: there were only four new grade ones. When we arrived I called the teacher 'tannie', the older children laughed and I turned my face away from them, hiding my head, pressing myself against my father, clutching his hand.

A few months after I start school our dog, Bruni, goes missing. We wait one night, and the next day my father and I decide to set out, to look for her in the area close to the forested slopes and the small natural lake not too far from where we live. This is an adventure with remarkable promise, as I have never been beyond the forest and the little lake by myself; there be dragons, I have been told. (Well, puff adders, to be accurate – not that we see any on this day.) Beyond the forest there is a stream of water – not quite a river – that rests for a bit in a natural pool before advancing deeper down the valley.

We call and call the dog's name, but there is nothing. And so, before we turn around to walk back for the hour or so that it will take us to get home, we sit down beneath an enormous rock overhang to eat our sandwiches. We are worried about Bruni, and my father is about to embark on an account of the nature of loss, and death, when we hear it: a faint, faint bark, from very far away. This comes to us on the wind, and if we were not exactly where we are – inside half a cave, really, which acts as a large natural sound-receptor dish – we surely will not have heard it.

We are presented with a choice: it is already after lunchtime, so do we return home and come back tomorrow, at which time Bruni may have moved away, or do we move on, into the mountains? Water is plentiful, there are mountain streams everywhere, but we have finished our sandwiches and there will be nothing more to eat. We probably have around four or five hours before sunset. My father decides to risk it. He asks me if I want to go home without him, back down the track we have come, but I insist on going with him. The faint sound of that bark leaves me no choice: I want to be part of this drama, of this good-news story.

We are lucky. After only another hour and a half we find her, higher up in the mountain, next to a rusted old wire fence. We are delighted, and it is a good thing too that we decided to push ahead today: Bruni is stuck in a trap. A wire noose is drawn tight around her neck, at a spot where she was jumping through the fence. The locals use such traps to catch small antelope for food. Bruni is lucky indeed: if she struggled, if she moved, if she obeyed her instinct to follow our voices when we called her, the wire noose would have tightened and she would have been strangled to death. We walk with her down to the nearest stream, where she drinks and drinks, too fast, vomits, then drinks at a more sedate, appropriate speed.

Nature has caught up with us, though, and in summer there are often thunderstorms in the late afternoon. We barely make it back to the large rock overhang when the heavens open, unleashing spectacular lightning and thunder. We know this will not last more than an hour or so, but we are afraid – and exhilarated. The lightning cracks and booms impressively between those mountains, echoing as we sit, huddled together, as deep under the overhang as possible. We are safe, but we do not feel particularly secure. My father smokes cigarettes and I hold on to the dog. I sit hunched up against my father, with my back against his front, looking out into the wild display. At last the electric drama starts to dissipate, but then the rain comes, a downpour, and we know we are going to be there for another half an hour at least.

As we sit there, waiting for the rain to stop and smelling that exquisite post-thunder ozone, my father tells me Oscar Wilde's story of the Happy Prince. Here it is: In a town where a lot of poor people suffer and where there are a lot of miseries, a swallow who was left behind after his flock flew off to Egypt for the winter meets the statue of the late Happy Prince, who in reality has never experienced true sorrow, for he lived in a palace where sorrow was not allowed to enter. Viewing various scenes of people suffering in poverty from his tall monument, the Happy Prince asks the swallow to take the ruby from his hilt, the sapphires from his eyes, and the gold leaf covering his body to give to the poor. As the winter comes and the Happy Prince is stripped of all of his beauty, his lead heart breaks when the swallow dies as a result of his selfless deeds and severe cold. The statue is then brought down from the pillar and melted in a furnace, leaving behind the broken heart and the dead swallow, and they are thrown on a dust heap. From there they are taken up to heaven by an angel who has deemed them the two most precious things in the city. This is affirmed by God, and they live forever in His city of gold, in the garden of paradise.

It is a beautiful story, and although I am sad I do not cry. We make it home in one piece, placate my mother, who at this stage is frantic, and build a fire, for a braai on our wraparound stoep. Within an hour my father is mellow and friendly from the wine, but no drama ensues that night. Instead, we talk companionably and enjoy being together, Bruni celebrating with a juicy bone. My father points out the constellations of the stars to me, and tells me about the double binary star system Capella, which orbits itself. Even then I understand how whimsical, how romantic this is. I ask him to tell me more about the stars, and how far away they are, but he tells me that my question is incorrect: it is not a matter of how far away they are, but how long ago they are. I tell him I do not understand this, and he says that what I am feeling – that sense of mystery – is God whispering inside me. Long ago and far away are one and the same thing.

Within a year we will move to Bloemfontein, where he is offered a job at the provincial arts council. As we count down the days before we leave our rural paradise, his drinking gets worse. While we are still in Clarens, though, he does not lose too much control. Near the end of our stay there, in early winter, my father takes me along when he delivers soup to a black family who lives in the shanty town just outside white Clarens. I see my father crying as he holds a dying man's head, tries to give him some soup to slow down the progress of cancer. A week or so later we move away, to the city, and towards the protracted and horrible end of our family union, tenuous as it always was.

The end was gradual, and then sudden, as these things often are. In Bloemfontein the only thing my father and I did together, our only father–son ritual, was to drive to a corner café in the city on Friday evenings, to buy fish and chips and coleslaw. We had a secret: we shared a small bag of slaptjips on the way home. In later years we often had such moments of closeness in cars, or on motorcycles. I remember him explaining Marxism to me, somewhere in the Cape, in a car during a high school holiday, years later. Another time he explained sex as a metaphor for lightness to me, in another car, before he smuggled me (too young for the state censors) into a screening of *The Unbearable Lightness of Being*.

When I was at university, we sometimes went running together in the vineyards, early on weekend mornings, before his marriage to Teresa fell apart. On chilly Cape mornings in the light mist he would tell me about the mysticism of Thomas Merton, or he would chant psalms that he had rewritten as rhyming quatrains. He told me about the shape of monastic gardens in medieval Europe, and explained the metaphysics of *l'art du vitrail*, and how it brought together principles of Christian and other eastern religions.

Even our very last friendly conversation, late in the afternoon on Friday 18 February 1994, was in his bakkie, when he fetched me from university to spend a weekend with him and Teresa and my half-brother. I had left him some poems of mine to read the previous weekend, and he was talking me through his impressions. He dismissed most of them, or complimented me in a way that let me down gently, as I was never any good at poetry, but there was one poem that really seemed to excite him. He seemed truly impressed, he appeared to perceive something beyond its surface that I did not yet comprehend, and then he gave me his greatest compliment ever: he told me that I was a writer. And he said that this was not necessarily a good thing. We smiled at this.

He is far away, and he is long ago. This is really one and the same thing.

SPLENDID IMPERFECTION

At age seven, I had grown tired of vehicular integrity. Or rather, the unsullied lines of sensible and expensive cars bored me. It was typical amongst my male acquaintances, at school, or for my two male cousins to declare their preference for a specific brand and model of motor car. This did not interest me much, and I knew nothing about brands and models. When, during school holidays, we were together in the same city, I would listen to my cousins exclaim their appreciation at a passing German or Italian car. I would say 'Yes, very pretty', which always seemed somehow to offend my cousins; the context-specific vocabulary and grammar of appreciation and delight seemed to elude me.

This was not restricted to cars or motorcycles; my cousins were collecting stickers of cowboys or spacemen, which were pasted into a book, but I discovered that I had incorrectly started to collect the female variant: stickers depicting the adventures of *Charlie's Angels*. My cousins laughed about this, and I put my book away. I always looked forward to being with them – as an only child I marvelled at their unspoken alliance and their sudden, violent wars, and I longed for this myself – but once I was with them, our different registers and rhythms started to wear. After a few hours, or a day or two at most, we were strangers to each other, we became polite rather than relaxed in each other's company, and we were all relieved when the time came to say goodbye.

Instead of admiring the bored perfection of sports cars, I developed an interest in the mangled shapes of cars that had been in crashes. Scrapyards were fascinating, and roadside accident scenes transfixing. When I walked past a car in the street that had a dent or a scrape, I would slow down to inspect it more closely. There was something about the unpredictable result of random violence that excited me. Instead of unblemished design, I appreciated the dramatic consequence of radical intervention. In later years, I discovered the same impulse in large art museums: the yawn effect of perfectly competent little watercolours versus the dynamism of Expressionism, or (though more muted) the more chaotic aesthetic of even late Impressionism. Abstract Expressionism (Rothko in particular) I find attractive; I enjoy standing close to these large paintings, trying to eliminate peripheral distraction, to feel the vibration from that ostensibly uniform colour.

But all of that was still ahead. At age seven, I was drawn to cars touched by violence. My father had recently bought a brown Ford Granada. It was a powerful machine, unfussy, with a deep growl and an indifference to what was considered pretty. I liked that. And as time passed, in the days and then in the weeks after the car was acquired and stood there, shiny and inviting in the same spot beneath the Clarens wisteria, bees floating by, I eyed and gradually became increasingly interested in those perfect, bold red brake lights at the rear.

As my parents conversed, on the stoep or inside in the kitchen, I amused myself outside. I made roads for my toy cars in the dirt road outside our property. As I moved the rocks or my cars along the dirt paths, I watched my father's car in the distance. My eyes moved over the cream roof and down the back window slope, down to the brown boot, over the edge and straight down to the rear lights. I observed the rounding of the large red light cover, as it passed from the back of the car to the side, and there it met the orange indicator light. It was very beautiful.

One weekend, when the feeling demanded expression, as my father emerged from the house with raw meat, about to get started on the braai, I smiled up at him. I was standing next to the Granada, my head well above the car boot level, and touched the red back light carefully with my hand.

'Daddy,' I said. My father stopped and looked down at me, the tray of red meat in his hands.

'Not now, Paul, I have to get this on the fire,' he said.

'Can I break the light, please?' I asked, as my father was about to walk away. He stopped, turned to face me, and looked to see if I was serious.

'If you break that light, I will be very angry.'

I nodded, looked down, and my father walked away. I picked up a rock from the heap of stones near the entrance gate. I took my time to select a spot that would allow the most promising results. When the first blow had no visible effect, I lifted it again, and struck harder. The glass still did not break; instead, there was a solid and spectacular series of cracks that ran in different directions, outwards from the point of impact. I was staring so hard at what I had achieved that I was not even aware of my father until I discovered myself being dragged by the arm in the direction of the outside shed.

'Why did you do it?' my father demanded. 'I told you not to do it,' he said loudly.

I shrugged. 'I wanted to know what it would look like.'

My father removed his belt and ordered me to bend over and hold on to the metal pipe that ran parallel to the shed floor. The hiding itself was perfunctory, a few lashes only, and not particularly painful.

I understood the utility of the punishment, cried real tears, and spoke the appropriate words of contrition.

I was not sorry about what I had done. I never vandalised another car.

THINGS MY GRANDMOTHER STOLE FROM ME

If I wanted to, I could tell you about the things my father's mother stole from me. But I do not want to.

I will not tell you about the birthday cake ('farm' theme) that she promised to make herself, for my seventh birthday. She forgot to remove the price from the box, the name of the bakery, and the 'eat by' reminder, and then insisted on the lie, when I asked her about it. I refused to eat any of it.

I will not tell you about the fancy toy car – a shiny, expensive auburn Citroën – that I saved for myself, over many months, and that she then took from me on the first day of my ownership of it. She displayed it in her locked glass cabinet in her formal lounge, 'to show me how much she loved me'. I was allowed to look at it once a day, when I visited her – but I was not allowed to touch it or to play with it ever again. I never asked to see it, to touch it, or to play with it ever again.

I will not tell you about the embroidered silk towel that my mother received as a gift – a parting token of gratitude – from an overseas choir she had conducted, which quickly went missing. There was one remarkably similar in my grandmother's large wooden chest (ivory inlay), which my grandmother kept locked. (But I knew she kept the key in the agate vase on the nearby table.)

I will not tell you about the call I made, hysterical at age nine, to her and my grandfather's house, begging begging begging for help in the middle of the night while their drunk son was assaulting my mother in a locked room nearby. I am unable to describe the silence when I asked her how long it would take for her to make her way to our house, and then her nearly inaudible sigh and that little click of the phone when she disconnected the call.

I will not tell you about the thin strong needle I used one week later to make a hole in her car's tyre, deflating it slowly, overnight, to make her late for an important meeting the next morning. Apparently even sweet grandsons can enjoy petty torments.

It would be improper for me to recount an anecdote from my father's childhood. When he was a teenager he witnessed a car hit a black pedestrian in front of their house. The pedestrian was drunk and the car was driven by a white family on its way home from church. My father was upset, told his mother what he had seen, and my grandmother asked him whether the pedestrian was dead. When my father confirmed this, my grandmother said 'Lekkerrrrr . . .', and kept that last guttural 'r' rolling for some seconds.

I will not tell you about the sense of victory when I declined her offer, delivered by phone, to buy me a car if I re-established contact with my father, when I was at university. She warned me that my presence or absence in her last will and testament was entirely up to me.

What I can tell you is that, when my mother – shortly before we fled my parental home in the middle of a winter night – expressed pity for my grandmother, for the children she had raised, a psychiatrist asked my mother whether she would also feel pity for a puff adder lying outside in the rain.

TREASURE

As a child I had a vivid inner life, and exotic fantasies. I suppose this is the particular privilege of an only child – especially a socially isolated one – though I gather most children have this facility. I did not require much of an external cue, though the adventures of Tintin, which my father bought regularly, to improve my English, and the arrival of television in South Africa, in the year I turned four, may have contributed.

One Christmas somewhere in the late seventies (I must have been six or seven years old), I received a shiny, illustrated edition of Robert Louis Stevenson's *Treasure Island*. I have it still; from where I am sitting I can see it on my bookshelf. This constituted the arrival of my treasure phase: for many months afterwards I was constantly seeking, boxing, and hiding shiny, precious things.

My parents raised me to identify and hold in disdain materialism in others. On my father's side, this originated from his own rejection of his parents' wealth, and their obsession with and celebration of material things (in brief, they loved things more than they loved him). Instead of materialism, I was taught to try to identify materiality – 'this is a beautiful thing, but what is its essential rather than its material value, and why is it beautiful?' Having said that, both of my parents were snobbish about bad taste, and material motivation as a vector for retail and purchase was deemed gauche, facile, common.

At the same time, great value was placed on things that held no or little material significance. The used pipe my father received as a gift from someone famous, the piece of string my mother wore, for many months, around her finger, when they were unable to afford an engagement ring, my disgustingly disintegrating first infant dummy, my dead maternal grandmother's worthless costume jewellery, which she had worn in small-town plays as a young woman, the little stones (gravel, agate, rose quartz) that I picked up wherever I went, as a toddler.

One day late in the seventies, in Bloemfontein, I gather all these things and add to them whatever banknotes and coins I am able to find in my parents' purses, and I place this in a small ornate wooden box, which my mother's grandfather carved and inlaid with bone, as a proxy for ivory, while he was an Anglo-Boer War POW on Ceylon at the turn of the century. The last items I add are two tiny, shiny rings from around the leg of a dead racing pigeon I found at the side of the road, on my way home from school, and two large, heavy one crown coins, beautifully crafted in fine silver, made to commemorate the royal family's visit in the late forties. In objective, materialistic terms, the crown coins and the box itself are the most precious items.

When my parents work, during the week, the house and the garden belong to me and to Evelina, who keeps the house, and an eye on me. In the afternoons Evelina often visits with friends working at neighbouring properties, and so I have supreme, splendid privacy when I take the small box and its contents into the garden. The garden fork is unwieldy, so I dig a deep hole with a small hand tool, as far down into the ground as my arm can stretch. It takes a very long time; multiple shifts of work over several days are required. My technique consists of two activities: first, I use the running hosepipe to do the digging and to soften the earth as much and as deep as possible, then I let the water dissipate, and do more digging into the soft wet soil. Eventually, I am happy with my handiwork: a very deep, narrow hole just wide enough to accommodate the box, wrapped in a towel.

Six months later, in winter, I want to retrieve my treasure, and I start to dig, day in and day out, in the afternoons after school, but I cannot find it. The property is huge, with a vast, leafy garden, and although I know approximately where I buried it, not far from the enormous loquat tree, the precise spot is lost. And now the treasure itself is lost.

My mother finds me after work, in the early evening dusk, sitting on my knees in a flower bed, with previously dug holes evident around me. She asks me what I am doing, pointing out that I am ruining my corduroy trousers, and I start to cry. I tell her what I have done, that the treasure is lost, but it is here somewhere. I am frustrated, I am contrite. I am very worried about being punished, but mostly I am devastated about throwing away our most valuable things.

My mother takes me indoors and runs me a bath. I do not remember where my father was; if he was there I would have remembered. I put on soft flannel pyjamas and when I emerge into the lounge Evelina and my mother are speaking in relaxed, friendly tones. I am allowed to sit on the carpet in front of the television and drink sweet coffee, and I am given melkkos with cinnamon and brown sugar – as much as I want. I start to relax, and my natural essential tremor switches to its lowest setting.

When I go to bed, our ritual is that my mother sits with me until I fall asleep. I cannot stand the darkness, so my bedroom light remains switched on throughout the night. My mother reads me a key section from *Treasure Island*. I listen attentively, but this time with guilt.

My mother closes the book, kisses me on my forehead, and before she sits back in the soft chair in the corner of the room, her own book in hand, she says this to me:

'Maybe the point of a treasure is that it remains unfound. A treasure is something that is never truly lost. It is simply where it is, unseen. Something can be unfound, hidden, but remain safe, still, forever.'

THE SHADOW MAN

I only remember the one evening, although it felt to me in later years that there must have been other such occasions. We were newly arrived in Bloemfontein, and my father agreed to a movie night. This was in the days even before video tape, so movie night implied a mobilisation of media: a sheet hung on the main bedroom wall; a projector borrowed from work, and an hour or so of intricate installation, involving metal wheels and bulbs. Reels of film were installed on top of the main machine, and once it all was in place, there was what felt like a very long time devoted to calibrating the various moving parts, adjusting picture sharpness, and aligning sound.

The room was rearranged to allow an extra mattress, on the floor next to the large double bed. To the side there were special dishes with a variety of things to eat, condiments, and drinks. The final touch was the adjustment of the ceiling light and bedside lamps, an invitation to darkness, and the shiver of excitement as the whirr of the reel got going. I was allowed to choose first; we would start with my selection, as I was expected to fall asleep at some stage as the evening developed, and then my parents would watch something else.

My father's presence was a rare event, and normally when he was home for an extended period of time and found a routine, it did not take long for our life together to find its dark default. But not this night. This evening we were laughing, we knew that the excitement and the warmth were to be cherished, and so we made the most of it.

As we were about to start, my mother discovered that she was missing something. There was a dish of sliced, baked vegetables still inside the oven that had been allowed to cool down and grow crisp. She asked for a brief pause, so that she could collect the tray from the kitchen and add it to the dip that she had made especially.

'Watch out for the shadow man,' I said, smiling as I lay on my stomach on the floor mattress.

My mother smiled at me, but as she got up to leave the room and walk down the corridor, the stairs, around the corner and into the sunken kitchen, my father stopped her.

'Who is the shadow man?' he asked.

I sat up. My mother and I looked at each other.

'We cannot see him, but he's always here, living in the corners and under the wooden blocks of the floor,' I explained. 'He's what makes the hair on the back of your neck stand up,' I continued, eyes large, towards my father.

He nodded, reaching for his cigarettes. My mother made a move towards the door, but my father held up his hand.

'And how do we fight him?' he asked.

I looked away, towards my mother, but my father leaned forward, close in front of me, to hold my gaze.

'What can we do?' he asked again.

I bit my lower lip and looked back at my father, because I knew the answer.

'We never walk around in the dark. The shadow man does not live in the light, we chase him away with it.'

'I see,' said my father.

My father was aware of my fear of the dark. At age seven, I still slept with the ceiling light switched on in my room. Later on, well into my teens, I would insist on the bedroom door remaining open, and a light in the passage outside. My grandmother – my father's mother – recently teased me about this, at Christmas, with my cousins in attendance. In the kitchen, later on, I heard her tell my mother that she was spoiling me, leaving the light on like that, indulging me, sitting with me until I fell asleep. My grandmother said that my mother was making me a moffie.

My father sat back, patted the spot next to him, so I joined him and looked up at his face.

'Tell you what,' he said. 'If you walk out this door right now, keep all the lights switched off, fetch the veggie chips and walk back here, without spilling any of it, I will make you a deal.'

I looked at my father. When I looked away, first to my mother, then at the floor, my father gently lifted my face towards him.

'If you do that,' my father continued, 'I'll buy you a motorbike when you turn sixteen.'

My mother said my father's name, but he held up a finger to silence her.

'But if you don't do this now, Paul, the deal is that you will give me your Scalextric set, with all the little cars included.'

I said nothing. My father was watching me with a serious expression on his face. I thought about the way to the kitchen. The house was enormous. It was completely black inside if there were no lights on – once, when my parents had an argument, I was locked out of their room, and stood in the passage, unable to reach the switch. I was there for a very long time, and there was no light whatsoever. The passage descended into the blackest black as one moved towards the kitchen. There, on the brink, one would need to climb down the stairs and take a turn, first left, then right, into the maw of the lower floors. And all the while, as I would have to walk down that corridor and down the stairs, and around those bends, and into the kitchen, I would know that *he* was there, watching me. The shadow man.

I shivered. I looked at my mother again.

'No,' said my father, this time more firmly. He held up a finger, then clicked on his lighter, compelling me to watch it. He moved the flame right between his own face and my own – an alignment of eyes, fire, and eyes. Then he extinguished the flame.

'I promise you that I'll honour this contract, that I'll buy you that motorbike, Paul, if you do this. But if you don't . . .' My father said no more.

I was finely attuned to my father's emotional field, and took the risk of a smile. I smiled broadly and then gave a little laugh, shaking my head.

'No ways, Daddy.'

After a second my father also smiled, with a closed mouth. My mother, to break the spell, asked if anyone wanted anything else from the kitchen. We said no thank you. She left the room, switched on the passage light, and I heard her walk away. No shadow man now, not with the light.

As I turned to sit down on my spot, to wait for my mother's return, my father (very calm, now, unhurried, warm) said to me, 'You do see what I just did, hey Paul? I tried to force you into an impossible deal. I asked you to do something you're really, really scared of, in exchange for something you really, really want. But I also built in a terrible price, in case you lost. Think about this for a bit, Paul; think about how people do this, out there, in the world.'

'I know, Daddy,' I nodded.

And I did understand. My father looked back at me, and as my mother walked back into the room, she saw her husband ruffle his son's hair, as fathers do.

'Right, Paul's movie first,' she said.

'I'll start the first one now,' my father said.

Then, with a wink, he said to me, 'Please switch off the light, son.'

DARKNESS GATHERING

In a way the interregna are the worst. Those periods – hours, a few days, sometimes a few weeks, even – of quiet waiting before the horror returns. Once, when I am eight or nine, during such a stretch of peace, everyone lets their guard down, we are happy, spontaneity allowed, as a family, my parents dancing together to something silly on the radio, Elvis, I think, and my father lifts his hand, in dance, mid-turn, and in a careless thoughtless instance my mother ducks, flinches, at that hand in the air, a muscle memory from a recent terror. The dancing stops but the song goes on, it is imperative to let the moment pass unacknowledged, but we all see it, and regard each other, and know what is coming.

MEANS, METHOD, END

The means was a large bag of glass marbles, the prize in a recent birthday party game.

I received the invitation on my desk at school: a party to celebrate a ninth birthday. The theme was 'The Wild West'. Arrived from out of town, one year before, I was still the new kid. By that time friendships had been established and factions formed, and so during school break I walked by myself along the concrete line that separated the lawn (*Keep Off!*) from the games yard.

The grounds contained various areas for rugby, netball, and other sports I did not know. I never ventured there; adults were less overtly feral than children, and so I stuck to an area as far as possible from the kids, but within sight of the windows behind which the teachers were smoking cigarettes and drinking tea, neatly divided into groups of men and women.

During break it was possible to do a circuit – one foot placed in front of another, heel to toe along the concrete line, turn, then back to the classroom perimeter – in about twenty minutes. As I walked, carefully, balancing, I would hum to myself and look into the middle distance, to appear nonchalant and unapproachable to those children, and unbothered and unweird from the teachers' window. Success meant no approach from anyone.

The only other person nearby was a boy called Ricky, whom all the kids called Milky. Ricky had a strange elongated head, blue veins showing, and thin hair. Something was wrong with him, and he avoided looking at anyone from behind his thick dark glasses. Not allowed into the sun, Ricky sat solitary under the roofed area next to the classroom doors, and during break time he ate special meals from a special container. No one ever bothered him. The party invitation was from Ricky, compelled by his mother to deliver a customised invitation to each of the nearly thirty children in the class.

The party itself was brief and tense. I was thrilled by the authenticity of my costume and Stetson hat, which my mother secured from the garderobe at work. But when I arrived at the party, this very perfection was out of place. My boots and spurs mocked the ordinary shoes and ankle boots of the others. My own accurate hat seemed showy and pretentious in the presence of all those straw sunhats and berets. Self-conscious, I pulled the bandana from around my neck and stuffed it into my pocket. Maybe, if more kids had shown up, I would have felt less conspicuous. As it was, there were only between eight and ten other children, and most of them were girls. What made it worse was that Ricky himself did not look at all like a cowboy. Instead of a Stetson he wore a crash helmet. Wild West indeed. I heard the mother explain to one of the other adults that the helmet allowed Ricky to join the children outside.

'You look great,' Ricky beamed at me, but I shook my head and took off the hat.

The mother was anxious. She choreographed everyone into what she called 'fun activities'. The children were self-conscious and bored, but the rules of a birthday party dictated enjoyment and compliance. And so we followed the instructions, the mother increasingly loud, increasingly desperate, enjoining everyone to have fun, not so fast Ricky, not so high Ricky, keep your sleeves down Ricky. I knew that there was no escape before the appointed time and so I participated in the games, although I did not understand group activities very well. I laughed when the others laughed; I tried to look anxious when the others were anxious, about the outcome of a game. And then, not knowing what was going on, I was declared the winner of an obscure activity, which resulted in my standing in the middle of a circle. Through some strange divination I had won a large bag of glass marbles.

There were five very large marbles, which the others admiringly called 'ghoens', there were ten colourless or slightly tinted ones called 'souties' (the most beautiful amongst which were crystal), and then there were thirty or so rather bland, normal little spheres with a twist of blue, white, and orange at their centre. I said the appropriate things about my prize, and smiled broadly for the camera. When at last my mother showed up to collect me, I thanked Ricky's mother, wished my host a happy birthday again, and left with the bag of marbles and a take-home hamper of sweets.

* * *

The method was based on patience and proper planning. I realised that, in order not to get caught, I needed to plan carefully, take my time, and not rush. And so, over the course of months, my plan took shape in my mind. I altered my walk home from school so that it took me around the school – the long way – out of sight of the main road, into a network of service roads that ran between the school and a power substation. From here I had a clear line of sight of the main school buildings about sixty metres away, on the other side of a brick wall. I was able to observe the buildings without being seen myself;

yes, the school windows all faced this way, but what I was planning would take place during the end-of-year school holiday. There were no houses or other buildings behind me which would betray my position. From here one could sit undisturbed and do the business calmly, with no need to rush.

I was old enough to understand that most of the mischief children were caught doing and punished for was done on the spur of the moment, resulting from emotional charge. Little acts of violence or cruelty towards others were the result mostly of reactions to an escalation of activity. If I planned carefully, I would not give myself away. I walked the way home, noting the openings of water drains at the side of roads, for the disposal of anything incriminating. Once the method was properly planned, all I needed to do was to wait until the holiday, several weeks away, and to be careful not to mention to anyone (to whom?) the means, or the object of my attention; I needed to maintain emotional equilibrium, demonstrating unconcern, happiness, calm.

I waited until the afternoon before Christmas Day. Those who had left the city for the holidays were long gone. The streets were quiet. Families were together, doing together-family things. And so I had ample time – leaning against a tree, steadying my hands, cap on my head (double utility: shaded eyes and an anonymising feature) – to shoot one marble after another from a rubber kettie into the air, across the school wall, the lawn, past the school pool and the games yard, and through the school windows. Over the course of what could not have been more than fifteen minutes I launched around thirty of the less desirable marbles, most of them hitting individual windows. I was amazed at the sound – that *ZING!* as glass encountered glass at great velocity – and the small milky cracks that burst around the holes. To my surprise none of the windows broke completely; there was no dramatic collapse of big shards. This gave me more time to regulate my breathing, and to move steadily from window to window.

At the end of it I knew not to linger. I walked quickly around the electricity substation, down a street and then turned into another. With a quick glance around I removed my cap and put it in a municipal bin. Near the corner with the next perpendicular road I looked around, knelt down efficiently and slipped the kettie into the gutter pipe. I removed a yo-yo from my trouser pocket and made a point of playing with it listlessly as I walked down the road, straining not to run. When I got home, I changed into other clothes. After a while my parents noticed me and put me in the car to spend the evening with my cousins and my grandparents. A week later, during our own coastal breakaway, I used some of my Christmas money to buy a new bag of marbles to replace the ones I had used.

* * *

The end was the feeling. That shimmer as I walked away from the scene, late in the afternoon on that Christmas Eve, as I sat quietly on my chair that evening where my grandparents arranged everyone around the family table, and as I sat on the plastic chair on my first day back at school, in assembly, as the principal deployed the presence of a uniformed police officer to scare everyone, as I affected the outward appearance of a thoughtful, quiet boy.

How delicious, to know what I knew, as the adults danced their little dance to reassert normality, the sense that they are in control, and careful, directed spontaneity. How fantastic at school, in that hall next to the others, to sit so still, to hear news of this violence, this outrage, this wildness that is amongst us all, and which would be pursued and eliminated. From behind my eyes I watched them. Not so indifferent now. Not so untouched. How powerful, this ability to command such strong emotion. How incredible, to hold this burning knowledge within myself, and to know I am the source of everything. How spectacular, to matter so very much.

You have no idea who I am.

* * *

Decades later, I visit that city for work. I sort of get it now, of course, processing it as an adult. There are words to explain it all. On the way to my meeting, I drive the long way, past the school. It is all smaller now, somehow, unsurprisingly. I see that same perimeter wall, that invisible area behind it, and that same row of windows.

I feel shame. I feel it genuinely, but also because I know it is proper to feel it. And still, from behind my eyes, I smile in solidarity with that burning boy.

THE DEVIL

I no longer believe in the devil, but I have seen him. I do not mean this metaphorically. It is possible that I was a little crazy at the time.

When we moved from Clarens to Bloemfontein, halfway through my first year at school, in 1979, my parents used the bulk of the money that my mother had inherited from her parents, seven years earlier, to buy a new car, and a large house in a posh suburb. My mother had, like my father, secured a management job at the Provincial Arts Council of the Orange Free State.

Our house, built on a corner plot in an old, established suburb at number 13 Morgan Street, had high ceilings and long, wide passages. There were several bedrooms, each of them with an en suite dressing room and bathroom, and an enormous sunken kitchen, which led to the pantry, and then to the garages outside. Between the kitchen and the living area (double-height ceiling, here) there was a dining area, and – pretentiously – a library and music room.

The finishes were in browns and orange, as was the convention at the time, with a large wall consisting entirely of thick frosted glass separating the living room from the rest of the house. There were many stairs, to different levels, and a heater built into the ceiling, in the main bathroom. The floors were either carpeted (the passages, some of the bedrooms), tiled with large blue-and-brown stone slabs (the stoep, the entrance area, the kitchen, the bathroom, and the pantry), or parquet (the rest).

The yard was enormous, front and back, with tall, mature trees and established greenery to enfold us in splendid isolation. In the front a gravel road swept in with an arc from one side and out another; in front of this was a vast terraced lawn, leading down to the trees and the perimeter dry-stone wall. At the back were several outbuildings.

It was an ostentatious purchase, but my father said things about investment and resale value, and so we moved in. The property was just over one kilometre from my father's parents' house, up the hill towards the oldest part of the suburb. Thinking about it now, it seems so obvious to me that my grandmother must have had a heavy hand in selecting and procuring the property; delighting in surveillance and control, our proximity meant that she could keep an eye on us.

We lived in this house for exactly three years, from July 1979 until the end of June 1982. That is one thousand and ninety-five days, during which I was aged seven until nearly ten. These were the years of my mother and my most acute horror. By the time we arrived in Bloemfontein my parents had been remarried for about two years. Prior to that, I have incomplete and emotionally neutral memories of my father; he had been mostly absent. The two years that he spent with us, once he joined us in Clarens, were not violent, as far as I can remember; he mostly slept, probably drinking, officially working on his new play. My mother by then had been shunned by her own sister and the extended family, for remarrying a political progressive; her own parents were dead by the time I was born, in 1972.

The thing about being seven years old and completely isolated from family, with no friends or acquaintances, an only child, is that you do not have anyone or any different context against which to check what is normal. Loneliness and feelings of isolation simply never come into

71

it, if they have no alternative. And so, when hell arrives, and is then sustained, there is no way to identify it as an aberration.

Instead, one is supposed to never *want* to fall asleep, because of what will happen in the night, when you wake to your mother's screams; it is *not* strange to develop an essential tremor so strong that you struggle to write, at school; it is the norm to eschew all interaction with the outside world, because no one can possibly understand what is happening inside the house, and the 'huisdinge' that are never to be spoken about. Your parents are beautiful, talented people, they work hard, there are great hopes for him in particular, to produce another play as acclaimed as the one performed three years earlier. Surely nothing can be unusual or too wrong if people recognisable from television glamorise one's lounge on the weekends: the tannie from *Wielie Walie* and her husband, who is the voice of Knersus, and also the well-known actors, the playwrights, the political lefties.

But then, after a while their visits wane. There are extramarital affairs. And when the affairs end, there is more alcohol and drugs, and escalating violence, and the names of mental health and addiction clinics such as Denmar become commonplace topics of conversation amongst the adults.

The violence. Snapshots, memories during this period:

– My mother, winded from being kicked in the stomach, doubled over on the floor, the monster laughing.

– My mother, neck cut with broken glass, selecting scarves to hide the evidence.

– My mother, neck swollen after being throttled, after having to physically pull her windpipe back into position, whispering on the phone that her voice is funny because she has laryngitis.

– My mother, blood in the whites of her eyes.

– My mother, her eye swollen shut.

– My mother, exhausted from standing naked on a table, all night, forced to denounce everything that defines her.

– My mother, telling me that maybe the two of us should drink pills to go to sleep forever.

Around that time, I report one afternoon to my mother that I saw a ghost hand come straight at me, from inside the bedroom cupboard, and that it feels as though someone is watching me all the time. After school in the afternoons I sit behind the curtain in the lounge, far enough from my father's room to not wake him up (please God), and I listen to serials on the radio, with the speaker pressed against my ear.

Around this time, my mother takes me to an assembly of the desperate, the sick, and the sad. We sit in an audience and watch a faith healer make a man's leg grow, and he stands up out of the wheelchair. My mother, while we wait in the queue to see the healer personally, afterwards, is approached by a woman, very thin, long straight grey hair and eyes wild, who points at her and then at me, and hisses, as if in Parseltongue, 'It is a demon; it is a demon.' We leave immediately, my mother laughing in the car. My mother tells me it is not the house that is evil, it is only us.

My mother takes me to a therapist. He asks me to make a drawing of myself. I draw a boy with long thin arms, no hands and no mouth, large eyes, with a shirt buttoned tightly to the very top, with many, many buttons close together. I understand something about madness. The therapist engages with my mother regularly, advises her to take me and get out, get as far away as she can.

I am so disassociated that I struggle to feel anything, and am only ripped into feeling when he strikes, and then the actual pain brings relief. I want him to hurt me, to beat me, to rape me, but he never does. I do not exist for him; only as a prop – when he needs to control my mother, to focus her mind – does he engage with me, does he make his way in my direction. And then she acts, instantly, to draw him away. But I *want* him to involve me. I am outside. I want to feel, I want to feel anything, I want to be included. Instead I am powerless, adrift somewhere behind my eyes. I am not worthy of involvement, of a beating, of attention, of a rape.

But this changes on New Year's Eve 1981. The events of that night will put in motion the end of our horror, and our liberation, our fleeing to a small Little Karoo town, six months later. And so the events of that night were worth it.

About three weeks earlier my father had returned from a month – a glorious month – in a clinic, somewhere north. Depression and anxiety was the diagnosis, substance abuse the symptom, and therefore not something he could be held accountable for. This was a sickness. When this diagnosis is delivered to me in earnest, grown-up terms by my father, I ask him if he would still have this sickness, and all these symptoms, if he were on an island, with no access to drugs or alcohol. He says yes, though I do not understand.

He starts to backslide almost immediately. How he does this I do not know, but he gets hold of alcohol and pills. The doctors predicted this, and so he is encouraged to use Antabuse, a drug which produces acute sensitivity to ethanol, and a hangover-like feeling immediately after alcohol is consumed. Combined with alcohol, it can lead to, amongst other symptoms, vertigo, blurred vision and confusion, even heart attack and death. My mother watches him swallow this every morning.

That Christmas, a few weeks after returning from the clinic, my father is ostensibly well enough to join us for a bizarrely formal Christmas dinner with his parents, along with my emotionally fragile aunt (also depression and anxiety, but no drug abuse) and her family. We all dress up in our best clothes. My cousins and I stare straight ahead of us as the adults have an alcohol-free meal, discussing the excellent progress that my father and his sister are making. My grandmother directs the topic and the tone of conversation, while my grandfather refuses to look at his children; when he looks at his grandchildren, it is with something between loathing and indifference.

My father gets worse after this social engagement, and during the week following Christmas he withdraws to a spare room, where he remains. Meals are mostly declined, he locks the door from the inside, and we talk in hushed tones, so that he is not disturbed.

My mother has a big work thing on New Year's Eve. Her boss is away, and she has to make sure that the New Year's Eve concert, in the newly built provincial arts theatre, goes according to plan. The concert starts at around 10 p.m. and will end at around half past midnight, ringing in 1982. Evelina is away, spending the holidays with her own family in Botshabelo, outside Bloemfontein, and so I am to stay alone with my father for the four or so hours that my mother will be away. This in itself is not strange; I have done this before. I have recently turned nine years old, so I am a big boy, and I can cope with this. Besides, my father will be put to sleep by the tranquillisers he has to take every evening after his meal.

Except that he does not take the tranquillisers. Instead, behind the door in the privacy of his room, my father swallows half a bottle of uppers with half a bottle of vodka. By the time the chemicals start to interact with the Antabuse, my mother is no longer home.

My first inkling that something is wrong is the sound of a crash, like a wooden crate falling onto concrete from a height, and something like a scream from the passage. I am at the time in front of the television, the cat on my lap, in the lounge half a floor below, on the other side of the house. I am watching a programme on the second-highest mountain in the world, K2, and my first emotion is annoyance, about not being able to watch the rest of it. I turn the volume down and listen.

The stench of my father's vomit hits me before I see him doubled over at the entrance to the room. The Antabuse is working to rid my father's body of the alcohol. He keeps on retching, forever, and at the end of it a large puddle of sick is gathered on and around his feet (he is wearing socks). My old friend – disassociation – embraces me, and I stand quite still, quite unemotionally watching myself watching my father. When at last he looks up at me, his eyes are blood red, and when he sees my expression he starts to laugh in a strange staccato way, with a high voice. I take a step back, bumping into Bruni. Her head low, the dog moves between my father and me. The room is now very quiet, with my father far away on the one side, and me on the other end. Bruni starts to growl, and I later realise that she was being protective of me.

With his stomach emptied of Antabuse and dinner, my father stands up straight, dead glowing shark eyes (red, from burst capillaries) instead of his own, and, addressing me, says my mother's name in a foreign, gruff voice, and 'Get into my room Right Now.'

This is his usual summoning of my mother, before a heavy night, and now I know that I am in trouble: if my father is hallucinating from the drugs, crazy out of his mind, and if he thinks I am my mother, then I know what will follow. My father lifts a metal pipe (a towel rail) into the air, like a spear, and then he turns it towards me.

'If you're not in my room by the time I get back, you will be sorry, bitch.'

He lowers the pipe and turns around, stomping towards the kitchen. I hear bottles crashing and cupboards being yanked open. My father is gathering half-drunk bottles of liquor from where he has hidden them, drinking as he goes, gulping down more uppers.

76

(It is quite odd to me, still, how alive I felt right at that moment. This was a music I knew, and although it was revolting, this knowledge, at least I was feeling. I was crying softly, afraid out of my mind, in hell, but also calm. That sense of viewing myself from the outside remained.)

I know that I do not have much time. My father will raid his hidden stashes (he is now outside, at the back, in the garage) for a few more minutes, and then the impact of the alcohol and the drugs on his brain will be almost instantaneous. My father does not get drunk or high like a normal person any more: everything is immediate, muscle memories and synapses lubricated by years of practice. I have between four and seven minutes to get ready.

First, I let the dog out. If my father feels that he is in danger from her, he will kill her. So I let her out the front, from where she quietly stands (attentive, but quiet, as this breed does it) watching through the glass sliding doors what is happening inside the house. I know that she will start to bark the moment violence erupts, and I am hoping that I can open the outside gates with the electronic system, from the entrance hallway, for people outside to be alerted to what is going on.

(Thinking about it now, I realise that it seems strange for me not to leave the house as an immediate reflex, and I do not really know why I did not. But rational thinking was beyond me then. Rational thinking belonged, then, to some fantasy world outside of the house, to a world so foreign that the inside of the house was the better alternative. Yes, it was a horror, but it was a horror I knew and understood.)

Now that Bruni is outside, I have maybe three or four minutes left to do a number of important things. I unlock the glass sliding door outside which the dog is standing, staring at me, eyes square and ears up. I then run up the stairs to the raised entrance hall, unlock the front door and the security gate, and hide the keys behind a potted plant in the corner; I do not want my father to lock us in. I then run to my parents' bedroom and remove the phone from next to the bed. I put the phone in a pillowcase, which I remove from the bed. My parents' two studies are near their bedroom, and there are phones in each of those rooms that I also remove and put in the pillowcase. There is one more telephone socket in the house, in the kitchen, but there is no phone installed there. I am hoping to get to the kitchen and plug in one of the phones there, and phone for help, before hiding in the empty kitchen cupboard beneath the sinks.

For now, however, I am stuck in the bedroom wing of the house, and in the distance I can hear my father move through the kitchen, back from the garage. He is opening the cupboards, drinking the cooking alcohol and (smart) eating something to line his stomach. He is preparing for a heavy session with my mother, whom he expects to be waiting in the spare bedroom. Considering my options, I make a run for my parents' bedroom, lie down behind the bed, so as to be invisible to a casual look from the door, and I plug one of the phones into the socket near the floor. I phone their place of work's general number (7-7-7-7-1), and the night guard answers almost immediately.

'PACOFS, SUKOVS, good evening, goeienaand,' says a male voice.

I try to control my breathing, and to lower my voice. I tell the man my name, and my mother's name.

'My mom is in the theatre complex, floor managing the concert. Please tell her that I phoned and that she needs to come home *right now*.'

I do not wait for an answer. I pull the wire from the socket and listen. The thing that is my father is walking through the house, switching on lights as he goes. He is swearing at nothing in particular, and at everything. I hear him walk into the spare bedroom, down the corridor, and he screams. He shouts my mother's name, Where the fuck are you, you'll be sorry, you better come out *now*, you fucking bitch.

My father is in the room with me. I can see his feet from where I am, under the bed, clutching the pillowcase with the phones. I hold my breath. He turns and walks out, shouting. I hear him move into the other side of the house, searching it from the furthest rooms. I plug the phone back into the socket.

'PACOFS, SUKOVS, good evening, goeienaand.'

'Did you give her the message?' I hiss, voice as low as possible.

'Look, there's a concert,' the man says, and I can imagine him shrugging.

'This is an *emergency*. She is in the theatre complex, managing the concert. My . . . There is someone in the house trying to hurt me.'

I slam the phone down and dial my grandparents' number (3-1-3-0-0-5). After an eternity my grandmother answers. I must have said something, because my grandmother says, rather formally, 'Peter-Paul, slow down, I can't understand what you're saying.'

I take a breath.

'Daddy is drunk. He thinks I'm my mom. He wants to hurt me.'

I hold my breath. I listen to my grandmother's breathing. She sighs. And then there is a click as she hangs up the phone.

I rip the cord from the socket, stuff the phone back into the pillowcase and listen. The good thing about a drunk is that they are loud; one knows where they are.

I run out the bedroom into the passage. Thank God for the carpet. I move quietly, and fast. But I misjudge my approach to the sunken kitchen and the entertainment area at the bottom of the corridor. I take the first two steps down too fast, and I slip on the smooth stone floor. I drop the pillowcase and one phone tumbles out, smashing on the floor. The sound is a thunder clap. The top part of the phone comes off and for a second I lie still, marvelling at the intricacy of the exposed wiring.

My father's voice – he shouts my mother's name, like a swear-word – reaches me. He is coming down the passage and so I roll over, off the stairs and onto the kitchen floor below. I stay down, crawl-ing across the floor towards the pantry, my head invisible to anyone coming in the entrance, obscured by the table top and work area in the middle of the large room. I hear my father fiddle with the bro-ken phone, then he flings it to one side. He's screaming. He storms straight ahead, into the dining room, and I move quickly into the pantry, next to which there is a telephone socket.

I plug in one of the two remaining phones, my father is now some-where in the front of the house, in the living and sitting rooms. Once he is done there, he will either come here, go outside, or head back to the bedrooms. The instant I plug the phone in, it rings.

My mother's voice is like a sharp blade. 'Paul? Wat is dit?' I can hear that she is very tense, very controlled. Her voice is coiled, almost someone else's, and the moment I shout 'Mamma, dis Pa,' I hear her drop the phone and run for her car.

My father has heard me, in the kitchen, screaming on the phone. I am already dead, and a great sense of even greater distance comes over me. It is almost funny. When I turn around, to check against my certain knowledge whether an escape route has magically appeared, I see the power box in the pantry.

The darkness of night was to me the epitome of everything evil. But apparently I was more afraid of my father, because I do not even think about it, I stretch out my hand and slam down all the connection points, including the mains, and the house is suddenly black. Outside I hear Bruni barking. My father is running towards me, coming into the kitchen. I ram the pantry door shut and in the dark I manage to lock it, with one motion, rip out the key, and stuff it into my pocket. I prepare to run, and as I do so, I can hear my father slip on his cold wet socks, skid across the kitchen floor next to me, and crash into the cupboard I was hoping to use, to hide.

But I know the house better than he does, and while he is swearing and screaming his way back into a stationary position, next to the sink, confused in the darkness, I am running perpendicular to him, away from him, into the dining room. Instead of following my instinct, to run into the lounge, I turn the other way, sit down on the floor, and cover myself with the curtain that hangs against the glass wall between the two rooms. I tell myself to breathe as deeply as I can, to catch my breath and to be quiet before my father comes to his senses and quiets down, in the kitchen. By now he has discovered that the pantry door is locked, and that he has no access to the electricity box.

It is pitch black, where I sit behind the curtain. There is a faint blue hue visible through the frosted glass behind me, coming from the sliding door in the lounge. Bruni is going wild outside. My father shuffles into the dining room, says my mother's name again, sounding exhausted. He turns the other way, into the lounge. I do not move, and I see his shadow right on the other side of the glass wall between the two rooms, as he scans the lounge with the little light coming in from the outside. Bruni is now barking so incessantly that I am able to breathe quite freely, where I am sitting, without the immediate danger of being heard.

And then there are car lights, illuminating the lounge from the outside.

My mother rips open the glass sliding doors and screams at my father, 'Waar is my kind?'

I saw a demon, that night, but there she is, an angel with the light behind her, shining, and I can see with my own eyes that, in all their terror, demons and angels are siblings.

When she inhales to repeat the question, my father strikes her with the metal pipe. She is flung against the glass doors and slides down to the floor, just as my father hits the door with the pipe, right where her head had been, smashing the glass into pieces. He picks up a piece of glass and starts to use it on her neck, and she pushes him away with her arms and her hands, trying to slide under the coffee table with her upper body.

I stand, paralysed, in the doorway, with the car light shining in my eyes from the outside. I scream a prayer over them, one that I have prayed before: 'Jesus, kill him! Jesus, please kill him!' and at this the dog becomes movement, stops barking and bites into my father's arm, refusing to let go.

My father, my mother and I watch in wonder as he staggers onto his knees, transfixed by the sight of the dog affixed to his arm. It becomes quiet, and we are all breathing loudly, my mother clutching her neck, my father staring at the dog, and Bruni growling very, very low. Eventually she lets go, takes position in front of my mother and me (me, behind my mother now), and my father backs out of the room, holding his arm, slowly moving towards the bedrooms, like oil flowing in reverse. We hear the key turning in the lock, and the sound of glass and bottles.

* * *

A few hours later, on the morning after my father tried to crush my mother's scull with a metal pipe, and then tried and tried and tried to cut her throat with a piece of broken glass, she stood on the lawn in front of the house, with a mug of hot tea.

It was cold, very crisp, and from my vantage point on the veranda I could see the hot drink and my mother's breath made visible, white cloud. The way I remember it, the image is completely static, except for the breath escaping her mouth, and the white wisp coiling upwards from the mug of tea. She is standing up straight, she has her side to me, and the morning light is beautiful. The light behind her hair shimmers gorgeously, mysteriously. It is very quiet; I do not remember any cars in the street, or any movement on the pavement. If it were not for the thick cotton bandage around her throat, held in place with little clips, the scene might be a painting, something created to capture beauty, by a contemporary Vermeer. In different circumstances, this might be the rendering of a woman enjoying her garden and the nascent morning light, she isolated in the middle of a vast lawn, drawing the observer's eye directly to her.

I refused to let my mother out of my sight, my father sleeping inside. Our priority on the day after was always to remain as quiet as possible, to let him sleep for as long as possible.

We did not know or have contact with any of our neighbours (pragmatic family protocols dictated isolation), but we knew that our neighbours on the one side were a High Court judge and his wife, a primary school teacher. I have no recollection of other children, ever, outside of school, but I suppose it is possible that they did have children living with them. On this morning my mother was in thought, pensive, trying to limit the movement of her head, the use of her neck, when Mrs Judge appeared at the verdant, overgrown fence between our properties. She must have noticed my mother from their side, despite the abundance of tall trees interrupting the view between the respective houses. It is possible, on reflection, that Mrs Judge was looking out for my mother, or for any kind of movement from our side.

The neighbour was in her nightgown (light peach) and running shoes (comical), arms crossed in front of her bosom, and said 'Hello,' softly, repeatedly, until she attracted my mother's attention. My mother stayed where she was, bowed slightly with her upper body, unable to use her voice. The woman gesticulated with her arm, asking that my mother come closer. My mother walked to within earshot of Mrs Judge, then stopped.

'Are you all right?' the woman whispered.

My mother said nothing, just looked at the stranger evenly. My mother's one eye was swollen shut, so she turned her working eye towards the neighbour. And thus they stood, wordless, for what felt like a long time. At a distance, I stroked the cat on my lap in the icy sun.

The woman then said to my mother, 'Last night I told my Dirk I think tonight that man will kill his wife.'

My mother did not say a word, turned around slowly and walked away from her, to inspect the evergreens on the other side of the lawn.

At that moment I began to understand something about outsiders. Mr and Mrs Judge were complicit. They were worse than the violent monster sleeping on the turquoise bedspread inside: they knew; they did nothing. A monster will do what monsters do. My father was simply being who he was; there is no pretence, no artifice about violence and destruction, about his very essence. But these people knew, and they did nothing. And this was not a one-off event. Their complicity stretched over the three years, the more than one thousand nights, the over one hundred and fifty dark weekends, for which we lived at number 13 Morgan Street, in that wealthy, leafy suburb. The prince of the law and the keeper of children knew, and did nothing: again and again and again.

There were others too who were complicit: my parents' colleagues, my father's parents, my teachers, the dominee – even gentle Jesus. I

84

had revenge fantasies about all of them. Later on, I practised stabbing them with knives, pretending that the gardening tools I played with on the front lawn were daggers that I stuck into them as they slept. I imagined hurting what and whom these people loved: taking their pets, or their children, just making them disappear. Or burning down their houses, with them screaming, trapped inside. Even then I knew what these fantasies were, I recognised their splendid psychological utility, and I kept them to myself. In truth I still loathe these people today.

* * *

My grandparents' car entered the driveway. They got out and my grandmother walked across the gravel road towards where my mother was standing, and remarked that the shrubs needed watering. My mother looked at her neutrally.

'Ai, jong,' said my grandmother.

My grandmother went into the house, and I heard a slight commotion from where I was sitting. She re-emerged and exclaimed that my father's forearm and hand were the size of melons, that he needed tetanus and rabies injections, but that the dog was refusing to let her get to her son to see to his wound. When my mother failed to respond, my grandmother snarled at her, snake eyes darting between her and me, passive in my chair, declaring in a loud voice that the dog was taking better care of her son than his wife was.

My mother and I started to laugh, which angered my grandmother. She said things I could not hear. My mother stopped laughing, and in a rasping voice she said to my grandmother that the dog was not taking care of her darling son, but guarding him, making sure he could not get to us. My grandmother opened her mouth to say something, but when my mother removed her bandage and turned her head and her neck towards her, walking to within a hand width from her, allowing her to see clearly, she closed her mouth.

'See what your son did to me,' said my mother.

At this, my grandparents looked at each other and walked towards their car. My grandmother did not bother to look at me or at my mother again, but when I asked from the stoep where they were going, my grandfather turned to look at me. And for the first time in my life I saw him for what he really was.

It was arranged that my father would return to the clinic for a more intensive programme. He would be away for two months. By the time my father returned, my mother had reached a strange equanimity. Without telling her in-laws, or my father, she had put the house on the market, and had sold it at a bargain price, but arranged to stay on until the end of June, so that she could find a job far, far away. By then my father was staying with his mistress, Vivienne, on weekends, so he was not there when on the last Saturday in June the removals van arrived and packed up all our belongings. By the time he got back to number 13 Morgan Street, the house was empty, and we were gone.

* * *

Fourteen years later, in May 1996, my half-brother Ben is seven years old and his mother is at a conference overseas. I am a student at university, and I am housesitting for Ben's mother. She and my father were divorcing at the time. She also asked our grandmother to stay in the house, to look after the domestic side while I took Ben to school on my way to university.

My grandmother and I were never close. After my mother left my father in the early eighties we maintained a civil distance, and had a formal manner with each other.

Towards the end of our house- and babysitting, the three of us – my grandmother, my brother and I – are at the breakfast table on a weekend morning. My grandmother breaks the unspoken rule we have never to discuss my father, with whom I basically had not had contact for just over two years.

'If only we can help your father be rid of the devil drink,' she said.

I said nothing. I was spreading jam onto a piece of toast, for Ben.

'He's not solely responsible for his life, you know. If your mother and Ben's mother took better care of him, in their marriages, he would be better.'

When she sees me looking at her, she hardens her position. 'Ja, he can take fifty per cent of the blame for his marriages, but no more.'

I get up slowly and I pick up the phone, which is near the breakfast table. I place it next to my grandmother.

'And now?' she asks.

'Now you phone my mother and apologise for the kak you just said.'

She glares at me. 'How dare you speak to me like that?'

I pick up the phone and I dial my mother's home number in Oudtshoorn. When she answers, I calmly relay my grandmother's expressed opinion to my mother. My mother goes quiet, and says that she will think about this, and she will phone later, to speak to my grandmother.

When I put the phone down my grandmother starts to talk.

'You can be angry if you want, but you know it's true,' she says.

'You are a disgusting *horror* of a human being,' I say, and sit down on the living room carpet to build a LEGO car with my brother.

She is about to say something more to me when the phone rings. 'I really, really think you should get that,' I say to my grandmother, without looking up.

While my mother talks to my grandmother, the old woman says

nothing. She sits quietly and listens to my mother for about five minutes.

When the call is over, she goes to her room. I phone my mother, who sounds quite calm, and tells me that, when I have completed my housesitting duties, I need never speak to my grandmother again. It is over. The puff adder will stay in the rain.

When Ben's mother arrived home I told her what had happened. She thanked me for taking care of Ben, and I picked up my tog bag and walked to the back door, to get to my car.

My grandmother was waiting for me at the back door. When she leaned towards me to kiss me, I took a step away from her and I lifted my hand and showed her the palm, as a traffic police officer would, to stop an oncoming car.

My final words to her were these:

'I can only imagine what it feels like to witness your own wrecked children, and to know that it is you who wrecked them. I will never see you or speak to you ever again. I hope you will have a long life, with many years, to witness the final collapse of the people you have made. And when you die, I hope you will be conscious. And in pain. And alone.'

I wish I could say that I am sorry about those words but, whenever I soften, I recall that clipped sound, that little sigh, followed by the click of the phone, when she abandoned me to the devil, at age nine, on that night. And although I realise that this makes me monstrous, that it makes me one of the devils she has made, I am not sorry.

EVELINA

My mother's father was a great admirer of Adolf Hitler. In photographs he can be seen emulating the Führer's personal style: same glasses, hair combed diagonally across the forehead, silly little moustache. The monochrome adds to the effect. The resemblance is striking, and this pleased him. He also hated Jews. This is ironic, as it was Ivor Rosenberg who gave him his first job out of school, when funds were insufficient for him to go to university. So instead he worked as a packer in Ivor's general store, in Brandfort, sometime in the 1930s, before Broederbond membership and the Afrikaners' state capture begat him the bank loans and the professional network he needed to purchase farms and livestock, and establish his dairy. In Free State winters he often developed bronchitis, which he blamed on Ivor's unwillingness to heat the shop. Later, while they were growing up in the 1950s, my mother and her older sister were not allowed to buy anything from Jews.

I suppose no one is really only one thing. It would be comfortable to dismiss my grandfather as just a racist and an anti-Semite. He certainly was those things – but he was also other things. My mother's relationship with him was respectful but uneasy; she loved him but often found him hard to like. His insistence on easy opposites – facile binaries – made her curious about the spectrum of greys between black and white, yes and no, ugly and beautiful, right and wrong. According to him there existed only these opposites, etched in moral and aesthetic clarity, and this had the effect that she increasingly shunned them, as she was growing up. My mother claims that this taught her empathy, and respect for ambiguity. This meant, amongst other things, that she chose to have sex before marriage, that she cut her hair short when he wanted it long, that she wore trousers where he prescribed skirts and dresses, that she smoked cigarettes, and that she sat with and held the hand of her transsexual cousin when no one else would, at his own mother's funeral. These choices seem obvious, innocent, and almost quaint now, but in the family household back then they were the cause of exasperation.

Such battles of the private were also part of a national darkness, as the white tribe's nationalism gained traction and institutional power. On Thursday nights no one asked where my grandfather went, but his car could be spotted with most of the other prominent men's near the school hall, where the weekly Broederbond meetings were held. My mother received an angry rebuke when she mocked him, only once, about grown men playing laager-laager. She refused the right that she had as a white person (at age sixteen) to sign the passbooks of her father's black workers, when they needed permission to work late or to walk through the white part of town. The most visceral moment was during her first year of university, in 1966, a few months before Verwoerd's (and her father's) death, when one of their workers, an old man called Mujaki, was caught stealing milk. My grandfather beat the worker so hard and incessantly that my mother witnessed her father, from the darkness of her bedroom, as he arrived back at the house, wiping his hands on the front lawn to clear away most of the blood.

But it was not all like that. My mother remembers with some fondness a time she was very ill, recovering from meningitis, when her father fried slices of biltong for her in a skillet on an open fire, and sang to her. How they – just the two of them – spent an anxious night saving lambs out in the open from a freakish blizzard, later bringing them into the house and warming them by the kitchen hearth. Those were good moments. Her father was an elder in the church, and she still finds it poignant that he died of a heart attack during a meeting of the church council – he would have liked to go like that. There were rumours that he had a wandering eye, and was for many years infatuated with the music teacher who taught at the local school. Still, he often picked a rose for my grandmother from their own garden, cut the stem carefully with his pocket knife, and to the end of their life together there remained a fondness and a respect that seemed inviolable.

Since both my mother's parents were dead by the time I was born, there remained only the extended family. But my mother's punishment for marrying, divorcing, and then remarrying a progressive artistic type was that she was shunned by them. Familial alienation meant complete material and emotional dependence on her husband, who rapidly moved the young family to the city. I can only imagine the scale of her loneliness when the young marriage collapsed due to my father's own infatuation and possible affair with a young academic. This presaged other dark things, and when his darkness truly took off, things looked bleak for her and her infant son.

Six or seven years later, my parents were remarried, but my father's failure as an artist fanned his pathology – and vice versa. He had by then abandoned the romantic pursuit of other promising artists, which meant that his philandering was increasingly unsatisfactory, and his choices became limited to less glamorous, more parochial characters – other failures. We were, all of us, stuck in a slow downward spiral towards something nasty and inevitable. The nightly tortures that he devised for his wife were becoming more and more violent.

It was into this dark place that Evelina Skosana arrived, in Bloemfontein, to keep house. She lived in a single room attached to the outside buildings, on the other side of the garden. She was a tall and ele-
gant young woman of more or less my mother's age, and although she
looked ridiculous in a maid's uniform, she wore it in a careless and
pragmatic way. She was distrusted by many of the other black women
in the neighbourhood, as she did things that culture frowned upon.
She smoked cigarettes. She rode a bicycle with a front basket, to buy
groceries. She abandoned the uniform and wore trousers. She called
my mother by her first name. When my father's mother phoned, occasionally, to pry or to issue orders, she refused to wake my mother to
come to the phone. She also knew how to read the vicissitudes of my
father's sobriety, hiding the car keys when necessary. All of this made
her an essential part of my life.

When my father's violence reached its apogee, sometimes I stopped
eating, and when I did not sleep during the night, Evelina kept me
out of school the next day, to sleep in her room. When I woke up she
taught me Sepedi words and phrases, and I taught her English, and
she took me to the park and allowed me to play on the swings while
other children from my school went to Voortrekker meetings. She encouraged me to make the swing go higher and higher, to be less afraid,
and rewarded me with little bits of liquorice, which she cut from long
dark strips with the small pair of scissors that she always carried with
her. She told my mother to stop fretting about my appetite, bought
me a syrup multivitamin supplement, and made me as many slap tjips
for breakfast as I wanted. When my father lifted out of his addiction,
he sometimes insisted on strangely decorous dinners, with multiple
courses, and Evelina showed me, winking, how to hide my vegetables
under the empty upturned half of a gem squash.

In the last year of our horror with my father, Evelina had a failed pregnancy during her second trimester, and she and my mother discovered with surprise that they not only shared the same brand of cigarettes, but also used the same antidepressants. They became very close, and Evelina decided that, if she could leave her own abusive relationship, my mother could finally leave my father. She helped my mother to devise and execute the escape plan. We left in my mother's silver Volkswagen Golf in the middle of the night, with my mother having lined up a job teaching music in Oudtshoorn, as far away from Bloemfontein and the Orange Free State as she could find.

We were giddy, as though we had done something thrillingly transgressive, and the first time we stopped was to buy petrol at Reddersburg, just before we crossed the Orange River and left the Free State province. As the sun came up the absurdity of the scene made us laugh: one small silver car, one black woman, one white woman, one Rottweiler in the back with the boy, potted plants, two goldfish in a bowl between Evelina's feet in the front, and a cat in the back window. Just before Colesberg the cat peed on my foot, which was in the kitty litter, and when I announced that the cat proceeded to cover my foot with sand, the women laughed so hard that we had to stop for a minute by the side of the road.

Those first few weeks in Oudtshoorn were the best of my life. We had been liberated. We were living in a small sandstone house in the poorest white suburb, and we were supremely happy. After those first school days we sometimes drove to Victoria Bay (the closest beach) and made a fire on the sand. Evelina saw the ocean for the first time and the three of us were transfixed by the sight of dolphins playing just behind the nearest breaking waves. My mother and Evelina drank cheap white wine, switched on the radio and danced with each other as I played on the sand with the dog. If other people saw us or disapproved, we did not take any notice. On the way back we stopped the car at the top of the Outeniqua Pass and illegally picked armfuls of wild proteas, which we used extravagantly to decorate the entire little house.

But Evelina had to go home, to be with her family in the Free State. We did not discuss the reality and the proximity of it at all, and on the day of her departure we simply drove together to the station, pretending that we were running an errand. None of us could speak when we got there; we simply loaded her suitcase into the part of the train that she was allowed to be in, and we held each other for as long as we could. My final memory is of running next to the train, holding her hand until it was no longer possible. I shouted Sepedi words at her, and she shouted back in English. I cried so much that I could not see anything.

I do not know if Evelina Skosana ever knew what she did for us, and how profound her presence and influence was back then, and continues to be in our lives. She blessed me with two parents – two mothers – in a time of desolation and chaos. She blessed my mother with a friendship – a partnership – so intimate, so sympathetic, that without it my mother would have disintegrated under the weight of her isolation. Before my mother saved herself and me, Evelina kept us sane, fed us, and made sure we were warm at night. She saved us from much more than my father. She saved us both from Brandfort.

CHRISTMAS 1982

It is five months since our escape from horror. We, just the two of us, cultivate a way of living without the monster. We are strong but we are brittle. We shun rules and reinvent them. At the same time, we crave to be the recipients, the objects of social rhythms and pre-dictability. It is very hot: somewhere over forty degrees Celsius every day, all of December; outside the tar melts into slow viscous toffee on the side of streets. By day we stay indoors, behind thick sandstone walls in our new rental house in the old part of a desert town we do not know. In the evening we open all the windows and the air from the Outeniqua Mountains changes direction; it brings a hint of the sea, right on the other side of our lofty horizon. We switch off all the lights and light candles on the stoep. The flames go straight up; there is no movement to speak of. Christmas dinner is whatever I want it to be. We have fish fingers with chips and mayonnaise. My mother sips icy white wine and moves her foot to the music from the record play-er inside: Kathleen Ferrier, Mahalia Jackson. We do not reminisce about Christmases past. (Two years ago, in the city, she disappeared for hours, came back, collapsed on the couch of people up the road, her face scraped, blood in her eye, she claimed she had walked into the loquat tree. It wasn't Daddy, she said, when I asked.) This year, after our meal, we get into the car and wind down all the windows.

The dog is with us, excited. We cruise through the town, slowly. One street after another. There is no one on the pavements. We pause outside the houses of people we do not know, for long minutes at a time, to observe them through their windows. Families at tables, families around decorated trees, gifts and wrapping paper, televisions, children, grown-ups. We can see them talking, their mouths moving, but we cannot hear what they say. At each scene, captured in ochre from our perspective as we drive, looking through those windows, we marvel at their ease. Ah, they look happy, don't they, Mommy, I say. Oh yes, they look very happy, she smiles.

TEETH

There is a secret compartment in my mother's wardrobe. I discovered it when I was a boy, at home by myself during flu season at school.

The wardrobe is an antique, handmade, and was bought with some of the money my mother inherited when her own mother died, in the year of my birth. I discovered the secret compartment by chance, when I inspected a wooden platform tucked beneath one of the drawers; I emptied the shelf and saw a dark wooden protrusion towards the rear. It had been painted black, the false bottom, rendering it almost invisible.

I removed the articles of clothing from the drawer, exposing a false bottom that slid away easily once you unclipped it from the back. When the cover came away there was revealed, deep inside the drawer, right at the back, a small cubed cavity laid out with dark-green felt.

The secret compartment contained the following:

– My milk teeth,

– What was left of my first dummy (rubber teat missing),

– A strip of photographs of my parents, somewhere in their early twenties, playing, pulling faces at the camera,

– A piece of costume jewellery – a cheap ring – that my father had given my mother when they started to go out, when they were fourteen years old,

– A pair of earrings that belonged to my mother's mother, Hester Agnes, and

– A yellowed letter from my father to my mother.

This last item was sealed (intriguingly, with wax), and so I was unable to open it.

The secret compartment was so magical, so whimsical, that I declared my discovery to my mother when she arrived home later that day. She was not angry about my snooping; she simply nodded and smiled, as though she had been expecting the discovery for a long time. She told me that the secret compartment is more or less the size of her heart, and that it contains the special little things she wants to keep in her heart.

'So this is where the Tooth Mouse keeps all my teeth?' I teased.

'Possibly,' she said, smiling back at me.

A few months before my discovery of the secret compartment, I had lost my last milk tooth. My mother and I had a game: I would put the freshly harvested tooth in my shoe, under my bed, and during the night the Tooth Mouse would collect it, leave me some money – and a letter, to thank me for the dental contribution. In the letter the mouse explained to me what the tooth would be used for: adornment of his house, or the crafting of an instrument for excavation.

But most recently, after the last tooth was deposited into my shoe, the night passed without an exchange for money, and no letter was left behind. The next morning the tooth was still there. I pointed this out over breakfast, expressing surprise, and concern for the mouse. I was not yet ready to give up our game. My mother suggested that I try again, that night.

The next morning the tooth was gone; there was some money, and a letter. In the letter the Tooth Mouse apologised for his tardy response. He explained that he was suffering from depression and anxiety, and that the medication he took for it made him fall asleep so deeply that sometimes his routine was interrupted. He assured me that he did not forget my tooth out of disrespect.

I read the letter to my mother at the kitchen table. Stirring her tea, giving me a shy smile, she rolled her eyes and declared that the Tooth Mouse's standards were slipping. I told her not to be so hard on the mouse.

My last milk tooth is in a secret compartment in my mother's wardrobe, with a few other things. The compartment is the size of a human heart, which is also the size of a fist.

THE AGREEMENT

Every year on the tenth of March, my mother would wait until about two o'clock in the afternoon, and dial the number. This was to a rural, farm line, so the call had to be transferred manually, at a local post office. My mother would speak the three additional routing numbers – 'twee, nul, agt' – and be told to wait. The phone on the other side would be picked up, with one short 'Hello?', but my mother remained quiet. Her sister (it was her birthday) knew who it was, and so, for seven years in the late seventies until the mid-eighties, the two sisters would sit quietly, saying nothing, and for fifteen seconds or so they would listen to each other breathing.

THE PRINCE OF NORDEN

I remember the exact moment you were born.

I was around ten years old and visiting my father in Pretoria, where he lived at the time. I was sitting down on the floor, flat on a thick carpet, playing, creating a world, using whatever was at hand – upturned ashtrays, stationery – deep in my fantasy, and I remember pausing, considering the game, thinking that I needed to adjust my inner life.

Until around that age, my fantasy worlds demanded magical things (magical thinking in the purest sense), often requiring the suspension of natural laws, mainly to allow me superpowers. But there on the carpet I considered all of this, concluding that I needed a more realistic and sustainable fantasy, from now on. I also wanted to establish a more enduring cast of characters, or one character in particular, whom I could take with me as I grew up. And so you were born, in a patch of sun on the carpet in what must have been a crisp cold Transvaal winter in the middle of a national and a personal State of Emergency.

What I am doing here is breaking a fundamental rule: I have never spoken to you, and you have never spoken to me. When, in the year I turned twenty-one, I asked a clinical psychologist whether having you in my life meant that I had a split personality, she smiled at me, assuring me that you are a coping mechanism only, a bit of play from my boyhood that has specific (and benign) utility.

You were such a practical creation: I could take you anywhere. No one would know. You could help me relax or project whom and what I wanted to be. Schoolroom orals became easy; I simply let you speak, my competent avatar. Previously I would sit in the boys' restroom, locked inside a toilet stall, and breathe deeply, deeply, to relax sufficiently to face the room. You took that burden away from me.

Whenever someone hurt me, or if I felt threatened, you were there to take it on, to defuse the threat. If a maths problem proved too much for me, I imagined you doing it, leaving me somewhere in the background, left alone to play, to observe, to think other things. You had such facility with people, and when my mother suggested that I work as a tour guide on an ostrich farm on weekends, to help with my shyness, there you were. You were always saving me, doing all the work for me.

That said, I do not remember you helping much during two personally stressful, existentially difficult periods. There was a hard time, around the age of thirteen, when I questioned my religious faith, or rather, tearfully expressed my suspicion that I lacked it completely. Both of my parents are religious – my mother conventionally and my father mystically, à la Thomas Merton, in the Christian tradition – but I lacked their trust, their certainty. You could not help me with that. And sex. When that became an issue, also very early on, I do not remember your presence in any way.

Not even imagined friends are perfect.

There was one amusing encounter with you – or rather, about you – that still makes me smile. It must have been in late high school when I reintroduced some elaborate metaphysics into my fantasy life. I made you do or experience something completely out of this world, and I paused, embarrassed by myself, because the fantasy was so implausible. I reflected, thought fuck it, this is my fantasy, I can do anything I bloody-well want, and relaxed.

My best friend and my romantic entanglements never knew about you, except for a girlfriend, at university, whom I did tell. I was so self-conscious, but she was kind, asked me questions about you, never mocking me. I think she found you endearing. Or maybe she found you – and me – ridiculous, but she loved me and spared me her judgement.

The psychologist warned me that you will feature less and less in my life, as I grow into myself and gain confidence. This is true. We meet so seldom these days, you and I. But when I think about you it is always with a smile, with affection and with thanks. I call on your echoes now and then, but it is more facsimile, more nostalgia, than real, these days; a fantasy of a fantasy, like a dream of a dream.

You remain, however, the best of me, my shining friend during much darkness, and more real to me than any metaphysics anyone has ever tried to foist on me.

We shall play again, I will call on you again, I suspect, when I am old. To that I look forward.

FINN

After our deliverance from domestic violence and chaos, when I was nine years old, my mother and I delighted for many months in indolent liberty. This freedom was existential rather than material. We had very little money when we arrived in Oudtshoorn, and there were many subsequent years of financial hardship. Toppers soya mince on toast for dinner every night for months on end. The same clothes week in and week out; a routine of hasty rinse and dry every night.

Previously, finances were never an issue, because of the money my mother had inherited from her parents. However, the price of our freedom was that she had surreptitiously sold the farm and the parental home, and then essentially given our expensive house in Bloemfontein away and paid off the mortgage to facilitate our escape. The merits of this transaction were never in question: my mother gave up material comfort and a satisfying management job, but she bought physical safety and emotional salvation for herself. And a childhood for me.

On the one hand, it is hard to explain to outsiders the specific dynamics of the alcoholic nuclear family. Tolstoy's 'all unhappy families', and all that. On the other hand, these kinds of accounts have been provided so many times that most people have a cinematically constructed sense of it. Anecdotes of physical and emotional savagery aside, let me make two points.

First: weekends were the worst. We were forever hoping that he would sleep, pass out for as long as possible, and for this reason any sound was deemed noise; it was our enemy. The house was permanently, desperately silent, and the rooms were kept dark. We spoke in whispers. The phone was unplugged, and the battery removed from the doorbell. I had to abandon cello lessons because they were sonically impractical; it would have been provocative of me to practise music with him in the house. Beware the ability of children from a pathological home to interpret body language, infer dark augurs.

Second: the tortured family becomes hermetically sealed – physically, socially, and emotionally. We were isolated not just from family, but as home visits were later unthinkable, friendships and even the most ordinary acquaintances were shunned. We never spoke about what was going on inside the house. If you look at my school photographs taken around that time, you will spot me amongst the others: the polite, slightly smiling boy; pale; dark circles under the eyes. That isolation and practised stance become first a matter of survival, and then the norm.

My mother has an anecdote of something that happened around this time: a colleague of hers and her own young son came to drop off something after work, on a weekend maybe. I noiselessly opened my parents' bedroom door a few centimetres, pointed at my father sleeping on the bed, and whispered 'See, I have a dad too.' I have no memory of this.

My point here is to create a sense of how dramatically different things were after we fled south, to Oudtshoorn. It was like moving from milky monochrome to LSD technicolour, from winter in Auschwitz to a Greek island in summer. Where I had been the solitary boy in a posh city school of well over one thousand pupils, wishing daily that school break would be over soon, I was now the exotic new arrival in a school of fewer than three hundred pupils. My rural school was in the poorest part of white Oudtshoorn, and my mother was the new music teacher and church organist.

My Free State accent alone, with its wide-open vowels, my fussy multisyllabic vocabulary (only child), and my proficiency in English (solitary hours with grown-up books on audiotape) made me an exotic creature – a juvenile unicorn – amongst the friendly, chaotic gang in that little community. This came with tremendous social adjustment – for the better. My mother was an instant celebrity, recognised everywhere she went in town. Children wanted to befriend me. I was cast as one of the leads in a school play simply because I could play the mysterious visitor from *Anderland* without needing to act or speak any differently.

In our rented old sandstone house, we ejected silence and embraced noise. We played vinyl records of Maria Callas loudly and deep into the night. We sometimes snuck into church on a Saturday afternoon and my mother played 'Bohemian Rhapsody', 'Singing in the Rain', and other secular works on the organ, just for my pleasure. We practised friendly shouting conversations with each other, me from the front stoep and my mother back in the kitchen. We ate whenever we were hungry, and whatever we wanted.

With our new, glamorous proximity to the ocean (only one hour to Victoria Bay), we often drove there simply to enjoy the dusk over the water, even on school days. We crept along the mountain pass that separates Oudtshoorn from the coast at absurdly low speed, because we were so unfamiliar with mountains. I was able to take my bicycle out of the town and onto dirt roads. I developed a tan. My insomnia improved. My tremor was less prominent. We relaxed. We were happy. We were safe.

I was not, however, a natural at recognising friendship and selecting companions. There had been no need of or apparent utility to them before. And so, a boy named Finn chose me and showed me the ropes. Established protocols did not at first allow me to be comfortable with him at home, in our space, so for a long time I went to him, to his family's house, rather than the other way around.

My father, when he discovered my mother and my whereabouts and came to visit, months later, admired our close friendship and suggested the name Finn, evoking a line from the song 'Moon River', sung by Audrey Hepburn – 'My Huckleberry friend . . .' – in the film version of Truman Capote's *Breakfast at Tiffany's*.

Finn's family was extraordinarily poor, even for that part of town. He lived in a tiny house with his parents, who were significantly older than mine (she, a homemaker; he, a former car mechanic). There were two older sisters, who had left school prematurely, still lived at home, and whose primary interests involved sunbathing and young men. They were a loving family, in an aggressive sort of way; it took me a while to comprehend that constant, loud scolding by the mother was simply a mode of communication. The father did not say much, and when he was not watching sports on the television (motor racing was favoured) he was fishing. After I met their whole family for the first time I came home and announced my great delight with them, expressing genuine amazement to my mother that there was a father who was around and physically present in the same room with the rest of the family, all day long.

They were all very entrepreneurial, in a tactile, practical way: the mother and the one daughter were forever knitting or crocheting dolls' clothing, or toilet roll holders, or toilet seat covers; the father and the eldest daughter were most often either fishing or caring for the four or five beehives that they kept on a nearby farm. I was slow, at the start, but my mother pointed out to me that these were ways in which the family was able to supplement the father's tiny pension. These people fascinated me, and I spent as much time as I could with them, observing them, reading the pulp picture books about hospital romance or military adventure that were strewn around the place. (My parents, even my mother, were snobs about such literature, so I never told them about those.)

It was strange that the Finns never used their capacious, barren backyard to cultivate vegetables. There were a few fruit trees, but they were seldom watered, and so the crop was nothing to speak of. Most of the space was taken up by rusting old cars, which Mr Finn had hoped he might fix, for a handsome profit. Finn himself could have done with some vegetables, as he exhibited what I later understood to be signs of malnourishment – mainly, he bruised easily, and his teeth were not great. My mother, once I started to allow him home visits, *chez* us, kept bags of apricots, oranges, and guavas in the kitchen, and whenever Finn was around she would feed these to us, sneaking them to us as dessert, or presenting them as treats, cut into wedges. Finn was never very interested in this, but he obliged her; at home they ate mainly bread and eggs, or sometimes fried polony. I thought this was delicious, but my mother explained to me that they could probably do without an extra mouth to feed, suggesting that I should discreetly make my way home before mealtimes.

Poverty and its progeny – humiliation – became a defining feature of Finn's life, and of the way he presented himself to the world. As we grew up, his anger about never being able to afford things also grew. The worst instance of this that I ever witnessed came when we were around fourteen years old. On weekends Finn worked at a video store, rewinding returned videos and doing basic cleaning; he was not as tall as me, so I was able to get the more glamorous job, as a tour guide on an ostrich farm. What money he did manage to save Finn used to take girls out, as he was always desperately in love. We also went to the movies a lot, and it was in the run-up to one such a cinematic evening that Finn discovered he did not have enough money to buy popcorn and a soft drink. He asked his mother and his sisters for some money, his mother was embarrassed, told him off for even asking her, and she then emerged from the kitchen cupboard with Plan B: a packet of Marie biscuits. Finn was furious, and there was a nasty scene with him throwing the biscuits across the room and rushing out of the house.

As he never had any money to entertain girls (despite the low-level pilfering from the video store's cash register, which I knew about, officially disapproved of, but secretly found thrilling), we had to entertain each other. Straight teenage boys are easy to arouse, and there are very few things indeed that they will not allow other boys to do with them. However, there is an inviolable line drawn at kissing – you can engage energetically and often in the most exotic kind of sexual discovery, but simple lip kissing is off the menu. It remains the acid test in burgeoning sexuality. Still, those were innocent times.

Not that Finn was precious about the ways of the world, or his own masculinity. In the weeks following his youngest sister's announcement that she wished to become a beautician, I remember crossing the main street in seething, mid-summer Oudtshoorn, noticing something strange about my friend.

'Finn, are you wearing make-up?' I asked.

'Yes,' he answered, unperturbed, timing his sprint ahead of an oncoming car.

Finn had a reputation for being a fantastic dancer. This is, I suppose, the benefit of having older sisters. He identified this as an opportunity for gainful employment, and offered to teach me, so that we could be invited to the matric dance two years and then one year ahead of our own, to dance with those girls who were unable to find partners. Looking back, this seems to me some kind of prostitution, but we had a good time and we did make a bit of money. The fact that Finn taught me ballroom dancing on our front stoep, with music blasting and a splendid view from the pavement and the road, did not seem strange to us at all.

My favourite memories of Finn come from our last year at school. His eighteenth birthday was early in the year, so he had a driver's licence long before I did. On Sundays after church we sometimes wore down his parents, or my mother, and borrowed a car to drive to Meiringspoort, on the other side of De Rust. There are spectacular rock formations, with cliffs on both sides, and if you know what to look for there is a small footpath that will take you to a high waterfall, at the foot of which there is a large pool of icy mountain water. Here we drifted on our backs, looking up at the magnificent Karoo sky, and smoked the menthol cigarettes that we managed to purloin from my mother.

Of course, there was no way Finn could join me at university, so our paths separated when I left, at the end of that year. We kept in touch, though, and during holidays we got together to gossip and reminisce about times past, but it was not the same.

I cannot eat an apricot, a guava, or an orange without thinking of him, and smiling. What I loved most about Finn was that he was so entirely himself, so unpretentious. At a time when I had to be convinced to leave the spurious safety of the dark, silent house in my own mind, he was there to thrust me into a boisterous, warm light.

THE IMPERFECTIONIST

Finn and I started to sleep together early in the year we turned fourteen. It was a great relief to us once this happened, once this was normalised, because our friendship had been suffering for some months – for more than a year, really – from a kind of undefined malaise. We had been inseparable since we were nine, when I arrived in Oudtshoorn from up north, but since the age of about eleven a tension started to emerge. There was no single reason for this; it was a confluence of many things.

On Finn's side, with puberty came vast love and fumbling lust for anything female, a more gregarious personality – or rather, persona – and increased frustration with his own family's poverty. Finn wanted to date, to go to school dances, to get new clothes – none of this was available to him, not really.

On my side, the elation at my father's absence meant the arrival of a strange psychological stasis. In hindsight I know this was depression – and its twin: anxiety. Existentially, this manifested in a loss of religious faith, which, in turn, fed my anxiety, and was, in turn, fed by my bafflement about all matters sexual.

And so, those months between roughly the ages of eleven and thirteen were dark and lonely indeed. Finn and I were misaligned, in terms of how we positioned ourselves in the world, about what we wanted from the world, and about the certainties about ourselves that we were cultivating. Although we remained friends throughout, we were not, until just after our thirteenth birthdays, as close as we had been before.

Even when we did become closer once again, we steered clear of trying to align our developing expressions or definitions of what was real and true. When we started to sleep together, neither of us considered the sex we were having, and the sexual things we were doing, as real sex – and certainly not as romance.

We did not view ourselves as lovers, and we were not in love with each other. We loved each other, sure, and Finn saw us and what we did together as the expression of close friendship: guys helping guys out. In fact, most of his narrative was about the girls he so devotedly followed, and desired. His attraction to them was genuine, obsessive, powerfully sexual, and to this day I do not think of Finn as anything but rampantly, demonstrably heterosexual.

As for me, I was in firm agreement with Finn: we were guys helping each other out. I was not, I can honestly say, ever in love with Finn. I loved him then and I love him today, still. I see him as a generous boy, then man, who helped me out, and who helped himself out. The one anomaly in this was the cuddling: after our teenage acts (brief, but intense, and infinitely repeatable, in a single night) we would end up, naked, glistening, one boy's head on the other's stomach, or lying next to each other, talking, arms touching, or flung casually across the other's body. There was an ease of being and of being with each other that was extraordinary.

Finn and I did not really discuss sexuality itself. We both knew that he was more exclusively into girls than I was. We knew of my little boy-crushes at school. We did not discuss any of this, not because we were too shy, or too unsophisticated to realise where our definitional selves were heading, but because all of that did not matter. On our weekend sleepovers we were simply alive in an undefined space. Now, I suppose, I can redefine it as 'queer', but back then such labels and the search for categorisation just never occurred to us.

As what we were doing with each other, and our friendship, was outside of the regular world, the things that Finn and I did with each other were also not viewed as cheating – nothing changed in our rhythms and ways of being together when Finn or I found girlfriends. Finn had a new girlfriend or crush every two months or so, with regular overlaps. I had fewer girlfriends, maybe two during all of high school, but the nature of my relationship with girls was more profound than Finn's. Finn was in love with girls and wanted to sleep with them; I was in love with them too, genuinely, but had little erotic inclination.

This, however, did not reduce my feeling of closeness to them, and I was, I think, not a bad boyfriend. I lusted after boys, though, although I had little desire to actually get to know them. Girls I loved and wanted to know; boys I did not care for tremendously, in terms of actual conversation. Later on, this would evolve into a vague asexuality towards both sexes; women remain so much more interesting to me, though: them I can know and want to know and be comfortable with; men, I am not so sure. Bisexual I am not, definitely, neither in equal nor differentiated desire or action; to me, the term is mostly useless. If you pushed me now, for classification, I suppose queer would be the word that gets the firmest nod.

None of this was close to clear, back then. At school, the objects of my affection were few in number – nowhere near as many as Finn's. For a year I desired Margaret, the pianist, in grade nine. In much of the following two years I was smitten with Cara, so beautiful, one year below me, and during my last year of school I adored Emma. Contemporaneously, though, across all of them and until the age of six-teen, my most prominent and venerated crush was a boy called Hugo.

Hugo was not gay; it would not have occurred to me then to factor that in as a variable. In fact, his very unavailability, his fey presence, was the thing that made him desirable. He was not one of those bor-ing louts, the posturing young men, little straight boys with pretty faces all wanting the girls. Those boys were lovely to look at, yes, but as sexually undesirable to me as a broom closet.

Hugo was interesting, though. A military brat, he lived with his parents and two younger siblings on the army base just outside town. Physically, he was attractive in a bland sort of way: dark-blond hair cropped army style; tall, though not quite as tall as me, bit of an acne problem, thick glasses from behind which he blinked at the world with very light-brown, transparent honey eyes.

My attraction to Hugo was based on how he carried himself in the world. Not outwardly smart (low marks for most subjects), he seemed indifferent to our day-to-day enterprise. But this was not the truth. He was simply indifferent to the human world. If you remained at-tuned to it (as I was), you would notice that he came alive whenever he engaged with or was in the natural world. He loved plants and birds, and at breaktime he sat with his sister to one side of the school grounds, speaking quietly, but focused mostly on the drawings of leaves or of birds that he was doing. Hugo got permission from the school secretary to gather up the used circulars and photocopy pa-pers from the allocated bin, bind or staple them together, and use the blank back sides for rough work and drawing.

By the time we were fifteen, Finn and I would sit on the school grounds near where the boys were playing soccer. Finn would join them, now and then, but I had no interest in doing that. I situated my-self in such a way that I had line of sight of what Hugo and his sister were doing. One day, when Finn returned, breathing heavily, from the soccer pitch, he sat back down, with his back against mine, and as we shared our breaktime sandwiches with each other, as we always did, he asked, 'Do you love him?' He nodded towards Hugo.

Finn did not ask this to hurt me, to expose me, or to put me on the spot, and he certainly was not jealous. He just wanted to know. I thought about his question while we chewed, and then I said, 'Ja, I think I do, a little.' Finn swallowed hard, chomped into the next bite (my food was always better than his), and said, 'Good-looking dude, but a little shy.'

I had become aware of Hugo a few years earlier, at the start of high school, during that period when Finn and I were not as close. I spent most of those days by myself, and I was determined to speak to as few people as possible. My routine after school seldom varied: I had no extracurricular activities, so I dawdled slowly in the direction of home, where my mother was teaching music to her private, after-hours students. We lived, then, about a forty-minute walk from school, and I had to go through the centre of town to get to our side – that is, the wrong side of the tracks. I could use a bicycle and complete the journey quickly, getting home within ten minutes, or I could walk. I preferred the latter.

In summer, when temperatures easily reached the high thirties and low forties, my journey meant a meander from one cool oasis to the next. These included the public library, the town museum, the pawnshop, the Catholic church, and then I sweated through the final four hundred metres up a hill to get to our small house, which was opposite the primary school where my mother taught.

I loved each of these stops: in the public library I would sigh extravagantly, quietly, to myself, into the coolness as the air conditioning hit me upon entry. My routine was to check for any new Robert

Ludlum or Ira Levin novels (although my mother insisted on reading the latter before I did – to scan for sections that were too sexual or graphically violent). I would then check for new music, amongst the small collection of LP records that the library kept. This is where I discovered the soundtrack of the musical *Chess*, which I kept taking out for months at a time, until the library complained.

The library also kept a tiny collection of dull, mostly faded print reproductions of what they called 'great artworks of the world'. This consisted mostly of Impressionist works. Occasionally I would take a print of a painting home, and we would hang it somewhere in the house for a couple of weeks. My mother was particularly fond of one specific Renoir, a scene of a path through tall grass, next to water. (Years later I took her to the Louvre, made her keep her eyes closed until she stood right in front of the real thing, and then allowed her to open her eyes. But all of that was in an unimaginable future.)

From the library I would walk to the town's main museum, which is right next to the library. The museum had a competent life-size reproduction of workers' houses and vocational studios, which I particularly enjoyed, and a large Big History exhibition with reproduced cave people and stuffed ostriches. This was all quite dramatic, although my real goal was to soak up as much of the coolness offered by those thick sandstone walls and the high ceiling. From the museum I would walk to the pawnshop, further up on the high street, to check on the acquisition of interesting knives and stationery. The owner was always polite, but kept an eye on his display whenever I loitered. Not that I blame him.

From the pawnshop I would turn into the poor part of town, and one of the side roads took me past the Catholic church, which was always open. I like empty churches, and the camp aesthetic of the Catholics in particular appeals to me. Sometimes (not often) I would light a candle and attempt a nervous little genuflection, on my way out.

It was on one such a day, a day of walking from one cool establishment to the next, that I first became aware of Hugo. I had varied my route slightly, went for a swim in the municipal pool not far from the high school, and as I drifted in the water on my back I heard a male voice, and kids' voices. I stood and looked across the pool, to where the sound was coming from. There were five or six children, maybe five years old. Hugo was teaching them how to swim. To the side sat the mothers, chatting to each other under a thatched roof lapa while they paid Hugo to teach their kids the basics.

Hugo emerged from the water with his back to me. He had demonstrated a shallow dive to the kids, and walked back to where they sat, watching him from the shallow end. He walked until he was behind them, then turned and faced my way, although he would not have been able to see me without his glasses. A much younger child – maybe a year old – had staggered from the mothers to where he stood, but he waved at the mother to relax, picked up the baby, and kept her on his hip, as he spoke respectfully and quietly to the children in the water in front of him.

It was the care that he took with them, the time that he was willing to spend with them, that made me love him. I saw this vital man-boy, two or maybe three years older than me, wet from the water, casually holding an infant and caring for others. Spending real time, giving proper attention – that is love. And I was amazed at his facility, at that age, to give such love. Physically, he was attractive: a swimmer's body, and a shockingly erotic line of hair running from his swimming trunks up his torso. But it was not lust I felt, not primarily, on that day; what kept me watching him was that ease of movement, of engagement, with those children.

I had more or less put that out of my mind when, an hour or so later, I entered the library on my usual route home. I nodded hello to the women at the front, did my usual checks, and as I neared the vast table where the daily newspapers were kept, towards the back, I became aware of him, sitting with a large book in front of him. Hugo – hair combed but still wet from the swim – was sketching something in a book, comparing his progress against another book to the side.

I collected the Afrikaans and the two English daily newspapers, tried to be casual as I carried them to a spot at a table from where I would be able to watch him, and sat down. Hugo never saw me, focused as he was on the images in front of him. After about ten minutes, he removed his glasses, rubbed his eyes, put them back on, and rummaged in his school bag, for something specific.

He took out three Wilson's toffees: one each of the blue, the black, and the yellow flavours. He let the toffee go soft in his mouth, then chewed it in a languid, silent way, eyeing the sketch in front of him. Then he took each of the toffee wrappers, twisted it around and around until it was a thin little rope, and made a knot in it. Without looking up, he took the wrappers and pushed them over the top of the books on the shelf right behind him, until they fell out of sight, somewhere behind the books.

He spent a little time completing some shading of his sketch with his fingers, then he put the sketchbook into his satchel, sighed, returned the book to its place on the low shelf, and left the library without a look in my direction. I waited until I saw he was on his bike, heading towards the main road, before I got up, walked over to where he had sat, sat down in his chair (still warm), and took out the book he had used. A book of birds: Hugo was making sketches of birds.

At school, Hugo was not good at anything, but now I knew he was kind to children, he gave swimming lessons, and he had the sort of inner life that brought him into a world where he could appreciate and make beautiful things. After that I did not see him often, at the library – maybe two or three times more – although I made a point of going to the pool when he was there. I also made more of an effort to keep an eye on him during breaktime, at school, which is when Finn became aware of him.

There were two other occasions when I was aware of Hugo. He was in the senior choir, which I was not yet able to join, and he was in the school's shooting team. Whenever there was a school event where the junior (standard 6 and 7) and the senior (standard 8 to 10) choirs would sing, I watched Hugo: second tenor, fourth boy from the left, third row. I noticed that he removed his glasses during public performances; apparently he enjoyed the singing and the practices, but hated the performances, and he removed his glasses to make the audience invisible. Clever boy.

Despite his poor eyesight he was a crack shot when he wore his glasses; he was one of the top two members of the school's shooting team. Apparently he did not enjoy this so much, but he did it to please his father, the Major. These were the days of our national State of Emergency, after the mid-1980s, and so on Tuesdays all the boys in the school were required to wear paramilitary garb, learn fascism, and play soldiers, marching up and down the rugby field. I got out of the worst of it by playing the trumpet in the small military band, and Hugo got out of it by going to shooting practice.

The school band (which became the military band, on Tuesdays) was practising in one of the science classes, towards the outer edge of the school premises, not too far from the shooting pavilion. One Tuesday, we heard some shouting and everyone found a spot by the window to see what was going on in the quad below. The shooting instructor was shouting at Hugo. Apparently he had been instructed to target practice by shooting at the birds feasting in the nearby school vegetable patch. Hugo quietly, firmly refused to kill or even frighten the birds. I remembered the boy with the sketchbook in the library, and nodded in sympathy.

The teacher screamed hard, all neck and vein, but Hugo calmly repeated 'No', again and again. The teacher became aware of his audience, two floors above them, and decided to escalate Hugo's humiliation.

'If you don't, I'll phone your father. Do you think your army dad will like having a son who can't actually shoot at anything alive?'

'I don't care what you do. I won't kill the birds,' said Hugo. 'You can punish me in whatever way you think is appropriate,' he added.

The teacher went very quiet, hissing things at the boy that we were unable to hear.

He shouted more loudly: 'Do you think you're perfect, that your splendid superiority doesn't allow you to do this?'

Hugo looked at him evenly and seemed to consider his words carefully.

'Sir, if I am anything at all, it's anything but perfect. I'm an imperfectionist.'

The boy smiled at the man in front of him; the boy was in complete control. The teacher went red, ripped the beret off Hugo's head and threw it on the ground between them.

'Give me your fucking glasses,' he spat.

Hugo took off his glasses and gave them to the grown-up.

'And now,' the teacher said, theatrically, for our benefit, 'now I want you to run at that wall, head first, and don't stop until you hit it.'

Hugo looked at the teacher, he blinked once or twice, turning to look at the wall. He looked back at the teacher and started to run.

He hit the wall with a dull, ominous sound that made us inhale. The band teacher screamed something from the window at his colleague below. Hugo lay on the ground, blood gushing from his nose. By the time both of the teachers got to him, he seemed to be conscious, and he was laughing at them. The shooting instructor opened his mouth, but the band teacher said something right into his ear, and he walked away. Hugo slowly got up and had to steady himself with one arm against the wall. He was magnificent.

My final memory of Hugo came maybe a year or so later. He had been suspended from school for a week, because he had taken a paper-weight – a beautiful glass object – from a teacher's desk. Sometime during that week of his suspension I saw Hugo at his usual spot in the library. But he was not drawing. His hair was still wet from the pool, where he must have been before, and he was staring at the bookshelf unseeing, without his glasses. He seemed very alone.

Word at school was that Hugo's father had been moved to another base, in another town, and so I knew this would probably be one of the last times I would see him. I approached the older boy slowly, so that he did not get a fright, and when I stood right next to him, he turned his face to me. It looked as though he had been crying.

'Are you okay?' I said.

'Oh hello,' he said. 'I'm fine, I've just been swimming.'

Hugo pushed his hand through his hair and showed it to me – wet. He wiped his hand across his face and put on his glasses, blinked until he recognised me.

'Oh hello, it's you,' he repeated, adding my name. I did not know what to say.

Hugo cocked his face slightly, to look at me properly, up close, and then he used his wet hand – or damp hand, rather, I suppose – and touched my ear. It was a sudden, gentle movement. I did not move.

'Your right ear is not the same as your left ear,' he said. 'The little flap bit on the top tilts down, like a tiny roof.'

He stuck out his hand again, and touched that bit of my ear, very briefly.

'Ja,' I said, 'when I was little my mom tried to fix it by putting cotton wool into that top bit, taping it with Sellotape.' I looked at him, then added, 'Didn't work.' I thought for a second, and then added: 'It's an imperfection.'

Hugo seemed to forget about me, dropped his hands down to his satchel, looked up and said, 'See you,' as he walked away. I touched my ear, where he had touched it, and imagined a bit of water still stuck there, from his finger. I touched my finger to my lower lip, watching him go.

Early the next week the school received news that Hugo had killed himself. There was a difference of opinion about whether the act had been intentional or not. The official story was that Hugo was cleaning his father's service pistol when it went off. But another boy, whose father was also in the army, told us that Hugo shot himself directly into the side of his head, at his temple. It could not have been an accident. In any case, there was no note. Apparently Hugo had been in treatment for depression, for some years. Acquaintances mentioned that, in the days before he died, Hugo had given away his personal belongings whenever he'd run into people he knew. Apparently this is quite common in such cases. But the official story was Accident.

The two school choirs sang at his funeral, and many of the girls cried. Finn asked me if I was okay, and I told him I was. There was an awful moment when the shooting instruction teacher memorialised Hugo by recounting what a good shot he was. I started to laugh, softly, on the choir stand, but Finn pushed me to sit down. And so I sat, on the stand, hidden behind the legs of the pupils in front of me, and softly laughed and laughed and laughed soundlessly until I discovered that my face was wet.

Later that day, in the public library, I sat on Hugo's chair, removed the books on birds that he had loved, and placed them on the table in front of me. Behind where they had been, on the bookshelf, I found a handful of Wilson's toffee wrappers, twisted and knotted. I selected a black one, a blue one, and a yellow one, and put them in my shirt pocket, over my heart.

Finn was very tender with me, during that month. And that Friday evening he stroked my back as I lay next to him. He did not quite know how to express it, how to care for me in a way that was appropriate, and so he asked me 'Would you like to cum?' I shook my head no, and said I wouldn't mind spooning for a bit.

Finn turned me on my side and lay down right behind me, with his body tight against mine. He pushed his arm under the pillow on which my head was resting, through to the other side, and there he took my hand. He hummed a bit until he fell asleep, and I felt both loved and lost, as I listened to him breathing.

THE EMERALD COUCH

When I am in high school I visit my paternal grandparents back in Bloemfontein. Those two savage, cold and wealthy people – cultural refinement carefully contrived – who only express what they call 'love' in material terms, as reward for material achievements. They bicker constantly, cruelly, but stand together like a pair of hunting predators when they instruct or remonstrate with their children, my father and his sister, or with their grandchildren. My aunt, then in her early forties, lies on a couch between their chairs, resting her back. (Something physical is always wrong with my aunt, accompanying her depression and anxiety.) Her parents are hissing biting things at each other, using fancy, genteel language, words like 'nonentity' and 'facile'. There are no raised voices – it is more subtle, more brutal than that – and we are all having tea together, from crockery so fine that you can almost see through the cups. As my grandparents administer their cruelty, I observe my aunt, on her side on that deep green couch, slip her thumb into her mouth.

STATE OF EMERGENCY

During my high school years, significant portions of my winter and summer holidays were spent with my father, first in the Transvaal, and then in the Cape. These were exotic trips, and mostly I looked forward to them. This was at the height of securocratic apartheid: a State of Emergency had been declared, the army was visible everywhere, and the townships were burning. My father was politically progressive. When he lived in Pretoria, I remember the thrill of smuggling affidavits out of the nearby homeland. These documents contained witness accounts of people being tortured by the security police, in the so-called independent homeland of Bophuthatswana, from where my father collected these affidavits (as a white person he was allowed to drive into and out of the homeland as he pleased) and delivered them to human rights lawyers. I remember being allowed to carry these documents in my backpack, walking the streets of Pretoria, as we made our way to the lawyers' offices.

In the middle of my high school years my father moved to the Cape and married Teresa. A medical doctor, she had given up a well-established practice in Kuils River and set up a medical practice in Mfuleni township outside Cape Town. She was the only doctor available to hundreds of thousands of people. There were intricate negotiations with the security forces, as Teresa had to travel in and out of the townships on a daily basis during a time when very strict security measures were in place.

I recall one particular holiday, in the summer of 1988. I was sixteen years old and Teresa was in her seventh or eighth month, pregnant with my half-brother. It was extremely hot – that white heat that seethes on the Cape Flats, with the wind blowing that relentless white sand fucking everywhere. One day a week Teresa was allowed to go into the deepest parts of Khayelitsha, to see people who were too infirm to travel to her relatively more safely located surgery.

We drove past the brown army vehicles parked at every major road into the township; the soldiers seemed amused and bored in equal parts. We drove on dirt roads that eventually became soft white sand, next to small streams of heavily polluted water, tin shacks everywhere. People regarded us passively, and Teresa and my father had little ramshackle conversations with the locals in broken isiXhosa and Kaaps. We had to walk the last hundred metres or so, deep into urban squalor, and there were what seemed like hundreds of children, friendly, milling around, touching our clothes, wanting to do no more than chat and tease.

Teresa was to meet with patients in a prepared shack, and by the time we arrived a long queue had formed. She was physically uncomfortable, enormously pregnant, but remained friendly despite the heat. She made herself as comfortable as she could in the surprising coolness inside the shack and asked for the first patient to be shown in. There was a minor commotion at the door, but eventually a man appeared with a small brown dog of promiscuous breed. The man declared himself healthy, thank you very much, and asked if Teresa would mind having a look at the dog. There was something wrong with its stomach.

Teresa paused and laughed politely, pointing out to the gentleman that she was really there to see human patients. The man remained unsmiling, and said that this was not a problem, as he was there, but would she mind having a look at the dog. He was genuinely concerned, and stood his ground, determined, despite taunts and heckles from some of the other patients in the queue. Teresa agreed. She gave the dog a rudimentary check-up, feeling its stomach.

'When last did the dog have a bowel movement?' Teresa asked.

'What?' the man said.

'Does the dog's stomach work every day?' Teresa tried again.

'What are you saying?' said the man.

Teresa sighed, frustrated, and made a sitting motion, asking 'Does the dog go to the toilet?'

It looked as though a light had gone on. Everyone fell silent. We looked at the patient's owner expectantly.

'O, dokter bedoel hoe *kak* die hond!' said the man, in perfect Afrikaans, triumphantly, understanding at last.

Everyone laughed.

The second patient was a woman of indeterminable age. She could have been anywhere between forty and eighty years old, to my young eyes. This is what poverty does: it strips you of dignity, hope, and all your markers of humanity. Age. Race. Class. Eventually even gender becomes difficult to recognise, at first glance.

The woman spoke very softly, explaining to Teresa that her heart hurt. She pointed at her own chest with both her hands. Teresa took her stethoscope and listened. It seemed fine, the heart. No, the woman insisted. Her heart hurts now. Listen carefully. Her heart is sore. Her heart is so very sore.

And then Teresa realised what the woman was saying.

'And what makes your heart sore?' Teresa asked.

'Worries,' said the woman. 'I have so many worries.' She started to cry softly and undramatically.

Teresa seemed helpless, did not know what to say. She asked everyone to leave so that she could see the patient by herself.

I felt upset, but I did not know why. My father lit a cigarette and started a conversation with some of the men outside. I decided to take a short walk. A few metres away from the shack there was a woman selling sheep's heads. It is a bloody business, with animal eyes staring at you with blue-white death. Flies everywhere. The heat. That white sand.

I walked a little further and felt the need to cry. There was nowhere to be private. Poverty does not allow for privacy.

Was this what the army was protecting white South Africa against? I could not see the dangerous hordes – the great black peril – anywhere. Instead there was a man and his dog, which was unable to shit, and an old woman with a sore heart.

'Nnnggg! Nnnnggg!' said someone behind me. I turned around. There was a boy of about my own age, smiling an open toothy grin. There was clearly something wrong with him.

'Hello,' I said. 'My name is Paul. What's your name?'

'Nnnnggg!' he insisted. Just then we heard the sound of an approaching aeroplane. 'Nnnnnggg! Nnngggg!' He pointed at the plane, jumping up and down. He was wildly excited, the plane was beautiful, and he wanted to show it to me. An SAA jet painted in those old orange colours flew over our heads, descending towards the airport two or three kilometres away.

'Yes, a plane!' I said to him, joining him in staring after it, pointing. It was the most beautiful thing he was able show me, his way of making friends.

I think about that boy often. I am embarrassed to do so, because I realise that the difference between him and me was mere genetic chance, and politics. We were the same age, we lived in the same country, but our lives where hemispheres apart. If he were white he would have been taken to the airport on weekends, to watch the planes take off and land, eating ice cream. If he were white he would not have been condemned by people who look and talk like me to live in filth, and only to see those magical metal birds pass you over on approach from one more preferable life to another. In a better world there would be no tanks and machine guns and military conscription to protect me against him. In a better world a much-deformed religion would not be allowed to cast us as opposites.

That evening, on our way out of the township, we picked up fish and chips and Fanta Orange, which Teresa craved constantly during the last few weeks of pregnancy. She was tired, after the day in the township. We crossed the highway that separated black South Africa from white. There was movement on the shoulder next to the road. There had been a car accident, lots of parked cars, emergency lights flashing. My father slowed the car down. Outside, on the tar, there was someone lying on their back, next to broken glass.

'How does it look?' my father asked his wife. She looked out her side window and answered:

'It looks dead.'

THE LINE OF BEAUTY

When I was young I loved a boy; he loved Jesus more, and left.

There followed a brief period of mawkish abstraction and counter-factuals, then life resumed.

The only physical remnant of our time together is a mixed audio-tape which, amongst others, contains a recording of the most beauti-ful piece of music in the world.

The first time I heard it was in his room. It was winter, and he had watched me eat the bean soup that he had cooked. He rarely had the student house to himself (I only ever visited him there twice), and on this Sunday he was keen for me to listen to something he had recently discovered in the university's music library. Holding the bowl with both hands, for warmth, I watched him fuss with the music system. Before he pressed play he sat down on the floor next to the speaker and turned his face towards me, so that he could gauge my reaction. And then it began.

First: silence.

The piece has begun, but for some seconds one hears only the ab-sence of sound. This is significant, and it is written into the score. Then a bell is struck. It is struck again, and then once more, and now the string instruments join and the sound unfolds. It proceeds from a sin-gle note, a single point, and, as white light contains all colours, this first note initially contains all notes, but disintegrates mathematically and methodically, edging lower, lower, until all possible sounds are heard.

There are words for what the composer is doing here, in music theory this is named, but one's initial response is purely aesthetic, elemental, and profoundly affective. This happens at a level outside of language or typology: when the dentist drills into a nerve, the brain does not first neatly classify the sensation as 'pain'; when one walks into the ocean and that first icy wave hits warm skin, one does not process the sensation as 'cold'. There is no time for interpretation, for reflection. Instead, that first sensation is *surprise*.

The brain needs order; it searches for a melody, a rhythm. This music offers neither. Instead of something predictable – a safe, comfortable template (verse, chorus; verse, chorus; modulation; chorus) – that first note tumbles down, down, in slowly repeating waves. The bell remains present, persisting in languid, relentless groupings of three, providing a counterbalance to the downward tumble. This is achingly beautiful, and very, very sad.

The absence of tune and rhythm means that the listener is unable to hum along; no rhythmic sway is possible; afterwards there will be no earworm. One has to experience this in a new way. The composer is doing something extraordinary here, on discrete tonal levels: the different string instruments play the same downward tumble, but on different levels and at different speeds. The result is not chaos; it bespeaks grief. Pure emotion, but expressed scientifically. This is a mathematics that bores into the heart rather than the head, although it is a creature of the head.

Near the end there is a chord that is splayed and held for well over one minute, as the tonal lines work their way back to a single note. And then, at the very end and in the very final instant, the bell is struck one last time. When the instruments cease playing, the bell's reverberation is the final punctuation. Silence returns, written into the score again, and it is over.

I hesitate here. Over-explaining this music – intellectualising it with anecdotes about the composer's life, or providing a theoretically precise account of his technique – may render it mundane, quotidian, and spuriously knowable.

Arvo Pärt, an Estonian composer, celebrated his eighty-fifth birthday on 11 September 2020. Artistically circumscribed during the Cold War, he left his homeland and settled in Germany, but he now resides in both Berlin and Tallinn. In the 1970s he devised his own minimalist compositional technique, which he calls 'tintinnabuli' (from the Latin '*tintinnabulum*', 'a bell').

The most beautiful piece of music in the world is entitled 'Cantus in Memoriam Benjamin Britten', and it is quite unique in Pärt's oeuvre. The composer is deeply religious and owes much of his style to the music of the sacred Christian tradition, but 'Cantus' is a wholly secular work, written as an expression of grief after Britten's death in December 1976.

I find much – maybe even most – of Pärt's work impossible to listen to. I favour his orchestral compositions over his choral works, although there is much that is sublime in both. My admiration of 'Cantus' has a lot to do with the manner of its entry into my life, and all that this evokes. I am aware that my response to this piece is driven by sentiment, memory, and context. But perhaps this is not problematic.

Maybe this is what art should do: remind us of our truer selves; reflect authenticity instead of artifice; surprise us with a strange echo from deep within.

For me, Arvo Pärt and 'Cantus' have provided such an accompaniment to my life: a place and an emotion I can return to again and again; a constant certitude; a line of beauty.

I PREFERRED MARTIN

I met Martin in the first week of our first year at university. We were eighteen years old, keen and shiny as new coins. I did an arts degree and Martin studied engineering. I loved words, and Martin loved music. Martin externalised his affinity for the arts more than I did: Martin sang in a prestigious choir, and on Thursday evenings after choir practice he went to the music library next to the conservatorium, to discover new treasures. I was less charismatic, more introverted, and held artistic aspirations within myself; I preferred the cadences and arpeggios of language to music notes.

I loved Martin, but Martin loved Jesus. He occasionally asked me to go along to a Pentecostal church, but I preferred the more subdued and thoughtful aesthetic of the Presbyterians. Martin and I were friendly, but in a way we could never just be friends. Martin made sure that he mostly met with me in the company of others. When we were on campus, during the daytime, we often ran into each other and chatted briefly, warmly, but only for a few minutes. In the short few years of our acquaintance, we saw each other without any other people present only twice.

The first time this happened was when Martin invited me over to introduce me to Arvo Pärt's 'Cantus in Memoriam Benjamin Britten', which he knew I would appreciate. Martin was making bean soup, chatting as he cooked. I liked silences, but Martin did not. Martin was telling me about mysterious things called Lagrange multipliers, and how they were useful in understanding objects that had massive volume but minimal surface area. I understood nothing of this, but enjoyed hearing Martin speak about it as he tasted the soup, added a spice, chopped a vegetable, rinsed a dish. I was very happy.

After the soup I followed Martin to his room, where he instructed me to sit down on the floor, so that I was in line with the speakers of the sound system. Martin sat down too and pressed play, observing my face. After we listened to it three times Martin ejected the tape and gave it to me as a gift. I still have that tape, decades later.

Martin then became quite serious, and told me about a recent weekend trip he had taken with some church friends, to the mountains nearby. Martin explained that on one of the evenings things had turned strange, and he suspected some of those friends to be cultists of some sort, or possibly Satanists. Martin asked me if I was a Satanist, and I said no, adding that I lacked the faith to sustain that kind of commitment. I laughed as I said this, but Martin did not laugh.

We both had girlfriends during our time at university. I saw and slept with boys and girls, but found sex itself disappointing. Martin seemed to eschew intimacy altogether, and mutual acquaintances complained to me that Martin seemed to become increasingly unknowable as time went on. By our fourth year I still wanted Martin, but I had more or less made peace with the fact that we would never be together.

The second time we were together – just the two of us – was on a warm evening about a month before our final graduation. I would leave soon to continue studies abroad, and Martin suggested that we say goodbye at the botanical gardens next to the old hall where Martin had weekly choir practice. I listened to the beautiful notes drifting out the front door to where I stood smoking beneath a tree. After practice, Martin came outside with the other members of the choir, laughed loudly at something someone was saying, and said his good-byes. He waited for the others to go before he approached me.

We did not really know what to say to each other. Yes, isn't it amazing how quickly these years have passed. Yes, I'll miss this town too. Martin seemed to hesitate – there was something he wanted to say to me, but he appeared to have some difficulty expressing it. I was sad, but somewhat irritated by the moment. So many years. So much dissimulation.

'I wanted to say to you, Paul,' Martin began, 'that I think you should be careful in life.'

Martin did not seem to be able to continue, but then he did. 'I think you should take care not to be so open. About things. About yourself.'

I was angry now. 'Look, Martin, I should go.'

And then, the extraordinary.

'I was wondering,' Martin continued, 'if you would mind it terribly if I gave you a hug?'

I was quiet. The anger was still there, but now there was also something else.

'Actually, Martin, I think I do mind.' I looked at Martin, turned around, and walked away.

A few years later, when I came back from overseas, I once saw Martin – still beautiful, still vital – from a distance, on a bicycle. Martin saw me, yelled 'Paul!', and we waved at each other. And he was gone.

Life continued. There was work, changes in profession, more studies, other countries, lovers, new cities. At least once or twice a year I would check the internet, to find out where Martin was and what he was up to. Nothing. No sign of him whatsoever. Not even on Facebook. Five years, ten years, fifteen years later an uncomfortable realisation dawned on me: Martin was dead. He was dead because he had killed himself. What else could it be? How can an engineer with a surname as rare as Martin's just disappear?

I based this conclusion on an anecdote that I had heard from another acquaintance. This acquaintance of mine told me that, before he came out, he was so depressed about who he was, and especially because of family and religious pressures, that at night sometimes he would drive to central Hillbrow, unlock all the doors and roll down all the windows, and drive through the worst areas very slowly, hoping to be hijacked, hoping to be killed. Suicide-by-poverty, my friend called this. His tactic did not work, and my friend has since made peace with himself, and is happy and in a relationship. I considered Martin's increasingly frantic religiosity, all those years ago. This, something like this, is surely the only explanation for Martin's disappearance. Martin killed himself because he was unable to hold those opposing forces within himself.

Still, every year once or twice I checked the internet. Nothing.

More years passed. I was offered a position at the university where Martin and I had met, all those years ago. Full circle. I drove past the house where Martin used to live and remembered that piece of music on a winter afternoon. I sometimes went to the botanical gardens to read, during lunch hour, and there I would see the spot where I finally walked away from Martin. I regretted that moment.

But then one day I was in the university library when, on a whim, I had a look at Martin's Master's thesis. On the acknowledgements page he thanked God and his parents. There was also the name of a Karoo farm. A quick search on the internet provided me with a phone number.

'Hello.'

'Hello. Is this Mrs _____? Martin's mother?'

A pause. Fuckfuckfuck this is cruel. To phone poor lovely dead Martin's parents is cruel.

'Yes? I am Martin's mother. Who is this?'

I explained that I was a friend of Martin's, from university, and that we had lost contact many years ago, and that I was wondering how Martin is.

'Martin's fine.'

Relief. He's alive. He is not dead. There had been no tragic moment. Still, the mother sounded careful, distant.

'I was in the same church as Martin,' I tried.

It worked. She seemed to relax. But I had to answer a few more questions before she allowed real ease to come into her voice. She asked me what I did, and when I told her that I was now a professor, she seemed impressed. Martin had visited his parents on the farm just the previous week, but he was then in a different small town, visiting with members of his community.

'Do you believe in Jesus Christ? Are you religious?' she asked.

There was only one answer conceivable in response to this. I had a sense that the answer to these questions was the passport to real knowledge, to real intelligence about Martin and his life.

'Oh yes,' I answered.

'So are we,' said the mother, 'and Martin is very religious. He has become much more religious than he used to be.'

She spoke to me for about an hour. I did not have to ask too many questions, to draw it out of her. She seemed almost relieved to be able to share the news with someone. There was much that was superfluous, but the pertinent facts were the following:

– Martin was alive.

– After graduation Martin became unwell (this was left unspecified), and received some sort of treatment.

– Martin left the treatment and rejected modern medicine and modern technology.

– He never registered as an engineer, despite the distinction pass.

– Martin now specialised as a kind of healer, sharing his gift with others in a small community based somewhere on the deeply rural east coast of the country.

Late in the call Martin's mother confessed that she was, privately, quite worried about him. It was as though Martin had become increasingly unreachable, and unknowable, as the years passed. She and her husband were no longer young, and although they would get a good price for the farm (a large energy company wanted to buy it for fracking), they also had three other children and a number of grandchildren for whom they wished to make provision.

Martin was living in a Wendy house, behind the house of friends of his, in a small town. What was to become of him? Trust in God was one thing, but she could not help worrying. She felt guilty about this.

I had gone quiet, it was as though I was in some kind of unreal place, when her question came to me loudly, via the handset:

'Would you like to phone him? He has a cellphone. I can give you his number?'

I wrote down the number on a yellow Post-it and pinned it to my noticeboard. I thanked Martin's mother for her time. I promised to come by if I ever passed through their part of the world.

I sat very still in my office and looked out the window.

The truth was that Martin was alive.

But that was not the only truth.

I remembered the shining boy in the green jersey, so alive on his bicycle, hand aloft, shouting my name – 'Paul!' – and the brave, terrified smile.

It occurred to me that my relationship with Martin had always had massive volume but minimal surface area.

I took the Post-it note with Martin's number from my noticeboard and put it in the wastepaper bin.

I preferred Martin when he was dead.

HINGE

The problem was a lack of authenticity. Or rather, an overbearing sense of immutable inauthenticity. Of course, I was familiar with depression and anxiety, but this heightened sense of what would later formally come to be identified as 'disassociation' was quite new. At the time I tried to explain it to my girlfriend Christelle as a sense of observing oneself coldly, almost indifferently, from the outside: even if you want to, you are unable to reach out and touch, to feel alive; it is as though one is at the same time watching and acting in a movie about oneself. And gradually you slip away even further, or deeper, and eventually you hear yourself speak, surprised about what you have just said, and wondering what you meant. You panic, or you want to, you would do anything to feel alive, to feel, to feel, to feel, but you cannot.

Christelle suggested that I see her clinical psychologist, a woman called Sarah, and so I found myself, on a Thursday morning in late May of my third year at university, riding my bicycle in the rain to a small office block just off Church Street, then climbing up a flight of stairs to a waiting room, and then seated, smiling at Sarah. After introductions and working out tentative protocols to do with seeing one's own girlfriend's psychologist, I told Sarah that I was there because it felt to me as though I had lost my way. Somewhere in my life the path towards the real me split, or disintegrated completely, and events then begat multitude different paths, each with seductions of their own. And now I was so far away from the authentic me that what remained of me was only an outline, a counterfactual of what might have been, of what should have been.

Sarah asked me if I felt that this left me with a chip on my shoulder, but I did not know the expression. I misheard it as 'chip on your soldier', but as I did not want to come across as stupid, I just said yes. Sarah asked me to give her an example of how this played out in my life. I was concerned that I had now committed to the soldier imagery, so I tried to keep my example as real as I was able to, without further blundering into a morass of metaphor. I told Sarah that I had always had a sense that my parents – both of them – were somehow disappointed in whom I had become. I suspected that my mother would have preferred a more spontaneously happy son, someone who would, say, walk across a lawn and then, instead of using the gate, jump casually over the low fence, the way confident young men did. I suspected that my father would have liked a more emotionally available son, someone who shared his own interests in words and books with him, someone more likely to sleep with many girls and smoke a bit of weed, or challenge authority in an intelligent way.

Sarah asked me to give a quick rundown, a chronology of my life up to then – just major events. I gave her an outline: the different cities and towns we had lived in, the schools I had attended, my parents' marriages to each other and (in my father's case) to others. She asked me to share a few key events, to demonstrate the alternative paths that I had taken, and which may have precipitated my sense of false trajectories and vectors. I answered tersely, providing only the most superficial detail. She kept pushing: another example, another example, another example. How did that feel? Why was that inauthentic?

What should have happened instead? I started to sweat. Why was this woman not getting it? Why did she keep on with her blah-blah about forensics? I was impatient, but I remained polite, and so I offered to write down a timeline, with key events marked along the way. Sarah thanked me for that, told me to do that, but she persisted with the verbal, she wanted me to talk about this. In the end I told her that I was unable to really remember what had happened – especially events before puberty. She nodded.

Sarah asked me if talking about my father made me uncomfortable, and when I nodded in the affirmative, she asked me to use words to describe the feeling. I breathed rapidly, a silent shallow pant, and I wanted to cry (although I did not). I shook my head. I can't remember, I said, I don't know what to say, I can't talk about him, I can't talk about those events. Sarah sat forward in her chair and told me that it's okay if I feel upset, that I was doing good work. I could feel her working me instantly, and so I retreated, I became unavailable, I willed myself into unfeeling. She sat back, made a note on a piece of paper, looked at me again. I smiled evenly. No tears.

Sarah gave me a box of crayons and a piece of paper, and asked me to draw an image that reflects my relationship with my father. I'm not much of an artist, I told her, but she said it did not need to be any-thing specific, no recognisable human figures at all, if I didn't want them, and that if she were unable to interpret the drawing, she would ask me to explain it to her. I reflected, took out the black crayon, and rapidly filled the entire sheet of paper with the colour black, except for a tiny enclave of white, maybe the size of a ten-cent coin right at the bottom of the page, towards the left-hand corner. I handed her the piece of paper. Sarah asked me what the colours represented, and I told her that I'm the white bit and that my father is the black bit. Tell me more, she said, but I shook my head. I don't know what to say, I whispered. I can't talk. My breathing was fast, again, and I was sweaty. She pushed, she suggested that I use single words, to describe the feelings, the meaning of the image. I shook my head. I wanted to leave. This was all a very bad idea.

I saw Sarah twice a week for six weeks, which we then relaxed to once a week, over the next two years. For the first two weeks my sessions with Sarah consisted almost entirely of relaxation exercises, with a slow and a gradually expanding conversation about the detail that I had been unable and unwilling to express at our first meeting. Slowly I started to remember, to feel, to name, to share. Sarah was carefully curating this journey; I was not alone; I was safe. She was teaching me that my journey – and my self – were not inauthentic, that there was no realistically ideal me, and that I should view the past (all of it, including the violence and the horror) not only as something that I had survived, but as part of what made me *me*.

After six months or so Sarah asked me to redo the visual image of my father and myself. I took out the black crayon and when I was finished the white blip had grown into a somewhat larger section of the page – not quite half of the page, but getting there. Sarah seemed pleased, but then she spoke to me quite seriously. Talking slowly, quietly, making me lean towards her, to hear her, she suggested that I may soon reach a decision point, a hinge in my life. My relationship with my father was changing, and I may soon have to make a choice about whether he was good for me, about having him in my life. She told me that this choice was mine entirely, that there was no right or wrong decision, and that, whatever I decided, she would be there to help me develop the skills to either manage my continuing close-proximity relationship with my father, or to manage my feelings and my sense of self if I chose to sever all contact with him.

Some months later, on 18 February 1994, this hinge arrived. There were two key events on that Friday. The first was the conversation with my father, in his bakkie, after he collected me from Stellenbosch to spend the weekend with him and his new family. As we were driving to their house, my father gave me feedback on some of my writing, focusing on what to him seemed aesthetically pleasing, universal, and true.

For the first time my father spoke to me as a peer, as a grown-up. I had allowed him to see something of my inner world, and in the process I relaxed the wall of ice that I normally maintained between myself and his world, which was the world of words and books. My father told me that he suspected I was a writer. This was possibly the greatest compliment he could give me. We smiled at each other and I think that precise moment was the most exquisitely, uncomplicatedly close we would ever be. Thinking of it now, that moment shimmers. My father finished this thought and said that it did not really matter what he thought, because in the end all children must kill their parents. Only later, only after, did I realise that that was our most perfect – and final – real conversation.

The second key event followed an hour or so after our arrival at their house. My father disappeared into his study and I was sitting on the lounge carpet with my brother, asking him about his LEGO creations. Ben had built a small city, all interlinked with roads, and he was working right then on an elaborate, abstract car. My father joined us in the room, which was vast – an open-plan space that incorporated the kitchen, a dining room, and the large lounge. My father walked past his two sons, into the kitchen area, and had a conversation with Ben's mother, who was cooking something for dinner. Ben and I did not pay any attention to them.

I asked Ben if I could see his new LEGO car, half-built, and he handed it to me, but I did not grip it firmly and it fell onto the carpet in front of us. The car broke into three large parts. I picked them up and I was putting it together the way it had been when my father spoke, loudly, behind me. He spoke in English, which he did when he was either being intense and intellectual, as he had been during our earlier conversation, or when he was drunk. At that moment it was clear that my father was drunk, or high on something; he must have spent the past hour or so in his study drinking, or taking pills.

'Did you apologise to your brother?' he demanded to know from me.

Before I could answer him, Ben said (in Afrikaans), 'It's okay, Paul'; my brother repeated this twice.

Something inside me broke. Not a violent rupture, but silent and powerful, like an explosion in space. I became very calm, turned around to face my father, and remained quiet. I felt different towards him, no longer afraid, no longer cowering inside, recalling the grotesque violence of years gone by. For a few seconds neither of us said anything, the only words spoken by my brother, who kept on repeating that the car was fine, and that he was not angry.

'Jesus, where's your fucking humanity?' my father said to me, turned around, and walked quickly into his study, closing the door behind him.

I gave my brother the LEGO car and reflected. The old me would say nothing, would be trampled and utterly destroyed. Previously I would take the energy of such an event into myself and park it somewhere abstract, then will myself into feeling nothing at all, floating in a syrup of inner grey. This event was a strange escalation, for my father: although he had done much physical and verbal violence to my mother, he almost never touched me or engaged with me directly when he was drunk.

I became very, very angry. But strangely calm at the same time.

Enough, I thought. Enough of this.

Without knocking, I walked into my father's large study. He was lying on his back, on a single bed in the corner. I asked him if we could talk about what had just happened.

'Of course,' he said, sitting up, turning to put his feet on the floor. He seemed utterly polite, and utterly sober.

'What would you like to talk about?' he said.

He sat forward, like Sarah when we were in a therapy session; he was reasonable, he spoke softly, as one would to a small child who had asked a parent the meaning of a new word.

'No,' I said, shaking my head slowly. 'Your behaviour was unreasonable and unacceptable. An hour ago, you tell me we all have to kill our parents, and now you want to play Angry Daddy with me.' I kept my eyes on him, unblinking. 'No,' I repeated.

My father sat back, now visibly angry, visibly losing control; he seemed confused. I remained where I was.

'Who do you think you're talking to?' he said quietly. 'I'm not your little friend, you know.'

I looked at him evenly. I waited maybe six seconds. And then I answered him.

'What are you then?' I asked.

My father knew better than to answer, 'Your father,' or something silly like that. He remained quiet, so I said again: 'What are you?' He blinked once, and before he could say anything more I turned around and left the room, closing the door behind me.

I kissed my brother on the top of his head and ruffled his hair; he looked up and smiled at me. I went into the room where I usually slept and picked up my unopened tog bag. Ben's mother drove me back to Stellenbosch. And that was the end of my inauthentic relationship with the man I call 'father'.

Now, nearly three decades later, I have an authentic sense of self, and I have the skills to filter and manage the debris of the past. I have stopped resisting the bad things. In a way, I think it is possible to change the past; not the objective facts of it, obviously, but their meaning and impact.

These days, not often but sometimes, I even jump over low fences, rather than use the gate. I find it good for my fucking humanity.

SONS AND LOVERS

My mother still loves my father.

For years he cheated on her, tortured her physically and emotionally.

There are shards of memory of that night – that terrible night – when he hit her with a metal pipe, then tried to cut her throat with a piece of broken glass. For weeks after, she wore jaunty neck scarves to work, in summer.

There were other nights like that.

And yet.

She has not laid eyes on him since 1984, nor spoken to him on the phone since the early 1990s, but he remains the love of her life. She never as much as went on a date with anyone else after their life together ended.

A few years ago, she had to undergo minor surgery, and as she started to wake up she was talking, confused. About how much she misses him, about how she often wonders how he is doing, whether he is safe.

Sometimes a song comes on, on the radio. It is from their time, from when they were young. She stops what she is doing, looks off into the light, through the kitchen window. She sways almost imperceptibly, to the rhythm of the music. She does not know that I am observing her. She knows better than to talk to me about him. I affect indifference, but the truth is that she is breaking my heart.

It is an extraordinary thing not to be loved by one's parent. There is something unnatural about it. Or maybe that is true only of mothers: perhaps 'to father' and 'to mother', as verbs, remain forever and fundamentally discrete, almost antonymic. Maybe it is not controversial for a father to be indifferent about his offspring. After all, my story is hardly unique.

In the year I turn eleven my father decides to study clinical psychology at UCT. He resigns his job, buys a motorcycle, and moves to the Cape. He lives in a garden flat, where I visit him. I think this is our closest time ever; he is very tender towards me. We watch *The Deer Hunter* on video, and we both cry. We take long drives on his motorcycle and he shows me the Cape. I daydream and sing songs in his ear as I sit behind him on the motorcycle, holding on to him with my arms around his waist, for hours at a time. We take the train to Simon's Town, and we take photographs of signs indicating that taking photographs is not permitted. Outside Durbanville on the road towards Philadelphia there is a short row of trees on the left, next to a fence. We stop there and he carves our initials into a tree with his pocket knife. I avoid that road now.

A few years later, when I am seventeen and he is married to Teresa, the township doctor, we go to a small café somewhere on the Cape Flats to buy vegetable soup with lots of pepper. The place has a good reputation for soup, and we do this often, during my winter holiday with them. My half-brother Ben is a baby, and in the front of the bakkie it is my responsibility to hold him. It feels cosy and warm, the three of us in the white Ford Bantam bakkie. When we come out of the café with the soup, a beggar sidles up to us, asks for money for food. We all know the protocol, the script. My father takes out a note ten times the usual amount in such scenarios, and says (meaning it), 'Man, los nou die brood. Gaan koop vir jou wyn.' The beggar looks at him in awe, and says, 'God seën jou, meester!'

Shards of life. Shimmering.

Four years later, I'm at university. My girlfriend, Christelle, is a fey person, a flautist in the university orchestra. I am her French tutor. Our relationship is intense, and for a few months I live with her, in a garden flat in an old, wealthy part of our old, wealthy town. We are inseparable, and we teach each other mysterious, private things. She comes from a wealthy family, she has a car, and this makes us mobile. On weekends we drive up and down the coast, or we drive inland, where we stay in tiny rural dorps. Life has great immediacy for us, we live separate from others, our orientation is inward. This is good and bad.

Christelle's otherworldliness is tragic; there have been suicide attempts. I am attracted to this. Her recommendation that I see Sarah, the therapist, is the beginning of the end for us, but we do not know it yet. Sarah is a kind, good person, and Christelle transfers to her partner, so there is no professional conflict. Christelle and I end our relationship, rather undramatically, later that year. My therapy with Sarah continues. A few months later my father and I become estranged. The break proves to be permanent. Sarah helps me through all of this. I feel better, more integrated as a person. The incipient sense of artifice that had been with me all my life starts to lift.

It is a year or so later. I have a new girlfriend, and I am happy. Therapy with Sarah ended six months earlier, but I receive a phone call from her. She needs to see me. I am delighted, because I miss Sarah. She is relaxed, and we chat as normal, for a few minutes, almost as friends do. She then goes a bit quiet, and she seems unsettled, tentative.

She sighs. 'There is something very difficult I need to do.'

I remain quiet.

'I've thought about this all the ways I'm able to, and today I need to share some information with you.' She takes a breath, looks at me. 'I need to talk to you about something that I have heard from another patient. I need to tell you something that another client told me.'

'Christelle,' I said.

She nods.

'Christelle has asked me to share this with you. She doesn't feel able to tell you herself, but she thinks you should know. And I think so too.' Sarah breathes in and out, slowly, pacing our progress, maintaining eye contact. 'I wouldn't do this unless I thought it was absolutely the right thing to do, morally and professionally. And I've thought a lot about this, considered all my options.'

I am not sure I want to hear this. I wait. I know I absolutely need to hear this.

'This may upset you very much, Paul.'

'Okay. I'm ready.' I am not ready for anything.

Sarah sits forward, towards me, and speaks softly.

'After your relationship with Christelle ended, your father remained friends with her, and with her mother.'

I know what is coming. I sit very still.

'Paul,' she paused, 'your father and Christelle have had a sexual encounter. At least once. She told me this herself.'

My mind empties.

'When?' I focus on my breathing.

'It happened after you and Christelle were over. A short while after you stopped seeing or speaking to your father.'

I say nothing. I hate Sarah. I hate everyone. I feel nothing. I want to throw up. I want to laugh.

'Paul, I'm telling you this because I don't know what your father

151

might do. I would rather you hear this from me, in this room, in this space, than from him, for God-knows-what motivation.'

'Are they still fucking?'

'No.' Sarah is firm, she shakes her head. 'I intervened. Christelle has no power against your father. She doesn't realise what he is. I contacted her mother. Christelle has moved back to Johannesburg – for now.'

I excuse myself and go to the bathroom. I stare at myself in the mirror and wash my hands, twice. I need the numbness to set in. I want to throw up, but I cannot manage it.

I see Sarah twice in the next week, then two more times, in the following month, and then I am fine, my equilibrium reacquired.

Shards of life. Darkness tamed.

A few weeks later, late in the evening, there is a knock on my door. I rent a room behind a house in a leafy part of town. I open the door, and there stands my father. I breathe deeply, but I remain calm. He seems desperate, feral somehow. By this stage we have not seen each other or spoken for well over a year. Before I can say anything, my father takes a revolver out of his pocket. I have no time to respond.

'I have nowhere to go. My marriage with Teresa is over. I've been driving around with this all day.' He motions towards the gun. I take it from him, quickly, I remove the bullets, which I put in my trouser pocket, and I put the gun in my cupboard. I ask my father to sit down. He sits on my bed and wipes his face with his hands. He is distressed, he has not shaved in days, he appears to have been crying. He seems brittle, and not quite sober. It is not alcohol; something else.

It is as though I am outside of myself, witnessing all of this as a disinterested party. There is a small play going on in my room. On a whim, I sit down next to him, and I tell him that it is all right, that it will be all right. I place my hand on his shoulder, then I slide it across his back and I hug him lightly. I am conducting an experiment.

'You've never ever done this,' says my father, motioning towards my arm around him. 'Never in your life have you embraced me.'

I remove my arm, not too quickly. I move slightly away from him. I offer him a cigarette. I am interested in what is happening.

'My marriage to Teresa is over. She wants me out.' He seems sad.

I am delighted by how little I feel.

Then he says: 'Paul, I slept with Christelle, you know. I slept with your lover. She came five times, I didn't come once.'

I make no movement. He is watching me.

'And where was Benny, while this happened?' My brother stays with my father at home, during the day, while Teresa works.

My father seems distracted by the question, vaguely annoyed.

'He was there, in the house, in a different room.'

'Ah,' I say.

'This had nothing to do with you, Paul. Absolutely nothing. I didn't do it to hurt you. I didn't think about you at all.'

This last reflection disturbs me. I am not quite able to identify the reason. I will only understand it later, after speaking to Sarah.

'Would you like a drink?' I ask my father.

'What?' He is puzzled.

'I don't have anything here – I don't use it – but I can fetch you some if you want?'

He lies down on my bed and when I return, an hour or so later, he is asleep. I put the bottles next to the bed, take the gun out of my cupboard, and put it next to the bottles. I check his clothes and the Ford bakkie, to make sure that I got all the bullets, and then I leave, to spend the night with my girlfriend. When I return the next morning, he is gone.

'What if he kills himself?' I am on the phone with Sarah. This is a few hours later.

Sarah is quiet for a few seconds.

'Then you respect his decision.'

I consider this.

'Yes.' I feel remarkably free.

If you put all the shards together you see a life. Every time you remember it, it is a little different. A detail here, a detail there. And a life can be a performative space. I am aware that I am over-disclosing, and that some of this may be in bad taste. I go too far, possibly. But I can live with that. As I have grown up, and matured, I have cultivated greater tolerance of human frailty.

Two years later, it is 1997. I am in Paris. I receive a hand-painted card in the mail. It is from my father. He has painted it himself, in watercolour, on one side. On the other side there is an extract, some packaged little wisdom, a quotation from the Upanishads. I make sure to read it only once, and then I burn it. I do not need this man inside my head.

Six years later, it is 2003. I am now in London, where I live with my boyfriend. I have a fancy UN job and an unhappy relationship. An envelope arrives. It is from my father. It contains three poems that he has written. There is a cover note. *Maybe this will help you understand. I am sorry.* I read this standing up, only once, and then I take it outside, put it all back into the envelope, and burn it.

I am not a kind person. I find it hard to forgive. No, that is not true. I do not know what it would mean to forgive certain things. My father's dalliance with Christelle damaged her – and him – more than it did me. Thank God Sarah prepared me for the news. This taught me the difference between rules and justice, between being correct and being right.

And my father? He is not – and I am not – the people we were when all this happened, all those years ago. He has been absent from my life for longer than he was ever in it. And I know that he is only a man; he was being, maybe, the only version of himself that he was able to be. I do not think about him much, any more. And now I am distant enough from him to make him art, or something like art.

My mother says that, when she misses him, or when she wants to give someone else a sense of his vitality, she thinks of Nathan, poor self-destructive Nathan, in *Sophie's Choice*, shirtless and manic, in that scene where he conducts the music on the vinyl record.

Me? When I miss him I try to think mainly of those moments with beggars, or with my brother as a baby, or when I was on the back of his motorcycle, long ago in Cape Town.

And even though I know – I know this for a fact – that he will never enter my life again, I cannot help, at graduation ceremonies, or at arts festivals, or during writers' talks, or casually on pavements, I cannot help but scan the crowd for the face of a man I last saw when he was more or less the age that I am now. I scan it for my own face.

All told, I find myself more respectful, more fond even, of all our splendid imperfections.

COUNTERFACTUAL

I am finally old enough for real regret. I am old enough to be losing the certainties I thought I had earned.

Thinking about it now, there is a handful of major Regrets. Real ones, with a capital R – not the petty, quotidian regrets of wrong roads taken, minor bad decisions, poor aesthetics, or little lapses in judgement. A typology of life: an assemblage of regret and Regret; action and consequence; love and fear; beginnings and endings – and having to live with it all.

Reviewing the regrets and the Regrets, and challenges at work and in life, someone who is wise about these things recently suggested to me that reiterations of the same challenge, or the same failure, could be life trying to teach me something. Life will keep on throwing up the same mud until I accept the insight it wants to impart. Life: lessons learnt and lessons refused.

One way of managing Regrets is to consider the roads not taken. Rearrange the shards, the mosaic. If we had stayed together; If I had been brave enough to love; If I had not pursued that offer. And then? Another life; another self, possibly.

I met her when I was twenty-one years old, a few months after Christelle's departure from my life. We were two out of twelve students in the same postgraduate class. Liesl lived in a student house on my walk home, and so we walked together, to campus in the mornings and from campus in the evenings, and then we had sweet tea together after every walk, and then we discovered that we were a couple. We remained a couple for three years.

We were not a natural fit. But the one thing we had in common – that fundamental need we both wanted to satisfy – was that we saw in each other the life that we craved. On weekend mornings we lay on her bedroom carpet, in our pyjamas, one of us with our head on the other's stomach, reading novels, eating soft white Marmite sand-wiches, drinking tea, smoking cigarettes, imagining what it is to be human, to be grown-up.

She started to read *Anna Karenina* and stopped at that magnificent opening line, handed me the book, observed my reaction. 'Happy families are all alike; every unhappy family is unhappy in its own way.'

'I'm the bit before the semicolon,' she said, 'and you're the bit after the semicolon.'

We both saw it: she was reaching past that semicolon towards my life, and was seduced by its spurious excitement; I was reaching past that semicolon towards her life, envious of its constancy.

We marvelled at the play-life we were constructing. She collected source material from the library and I wrote our essays. A few times we took my half-brother Ben (then five or six years old) to kids' mov-ies in the mall. *Power Rangers* at a Saturday matinee, the Spur for burgers and ice cream afterwards. An elderly couple looked at the three of us laughing loudly; they smiled approvingly and asked Liesl and me if Ben was ours. Afterwards, in the car, she looked at me and said, 'This is good, eh?' Yes, it was good.

At our kitchen table, once, she paged through a *Huisgenoot* and asked me where I thought I would be in ten years' time. I considered this and told her that I hoped just to be a good person, and live in the calm. She listened, seemed to disapprove, and told me that in ten years' time she would live in a home much like those in the *Huisgenoot*, probably somewhere in the northern suburbs, in a marriage that would be safe but unexciting, married to someone not unlike her own father. She will be a mother to a small son with his father's name, or a variation of his father's name, she will have a half-day job, something nondescript, and on weekends they will visit with her husband's parents, or with her own. That was the saddest I ever saw her.

Once, after we were reckless about birth control, we spent an early morning freezing outside a public health clinic, waiting to collect a morning-after pill. We went to a fancy restaurant for eggs Benedict and cappuccinos, and before she swallowed that tablet, she paused, frowned, looked at the tiny white round thing, and hesitated. She nodded at me, for confirmation; I nodded back at her. After she swallowed it we were quiet and serious, but she helped both of us with a joke, saying that this breakfast was definitely not good for the baby. We laughed a bit too loudly.

Towards the end, a few months before I left for Paris, on a whim we decided to become engaged, we bought a cheap ring, played at it for a week, then ended it. We were engaged – and then we were not. We knew how to play-act our happiness; we were happy, but we did not know how to face the looming reality, how to swop our photo negative for the sharp colours of real life. And so we ended it messily, haplessly, suddenly. She hand-delivered a letter to my small tutorial office, and kissed me quickly. From the sixth-floor window I watched her leave; I knew what the letter would say. I knew it was over, and that I would not see her again. In the letter she said that our thirty-six months together had been the happiest of her life, and she was leaving campus to go home, to her parents, she would not complete her thesis, and she loved me, and would I please be happy, and would I please not contact her because she couldn't bear it.

Liesl and I provided for each other cave wall glimpses of counterfactual lives, reflected in the fire of what we feared, and what we thought we wanted to be. We hid inside each other for as long as we could, to postpone the inevitability of our actual lives.

Her birthday is in late January, a few days before my brother's. A few years ago I found her on her employer's website and sent her good wishes. She responded politely, taking her time to tell me about her life. They have a son, he is twelve years old, her husband is a good father, they live in the northern suburbs. She is happy. Her Facebook page contains a few public photographs: a child, open smiles, a couple embracing. She does not seem so much older, although it has been well over twenty years. I study the photographs carefully. I try to figure out what is missing, and then I realise it is *me*. I am not there – and this could have been my life. It seems like a good life. I send a friend request on Facebook, but it remains unanswered.

She loved me. And I adored her. I love the life we had. I love the lives we could have had. I loved her very much – but not enough.

DEPRESSION

There was a time, not all that long ago, when going to the cinema involved a moment, right at the start of the film, when a projectionist had to make sure that, firstly, the focus was sharp, and secondly, that the image and the sound were aligned. If this alignment did not happen, the audience would become restless, annoyed, turn around in their seats and look up towards the unseen projectionist, voices raised in protest. On the screen the actors would speak, but the sound came too late, or too early – often only by a fraction of a second – creating a sense of unreality, unease, dissonance. That is how disassociation feels, and then the spiral downwards, inwards, until everyone else is behind water, and you are waving, invisible, in slow motion.

THE SECOND COMING OUT

Back in 1991, during my first year at university, my mother and I had 'the conversation'.

This is something most queer people dread: telling your parents what you are not, and then, what you are. Even the words available on the menu are difficult, unhelpful, making an open conversation tricky. There is so much you can be, these days, this side of cisgender, of straight: gay (well, not always), bi- (is that really a thing? – so many gays are nasty about this), a-, trans-, inter-, or something, well, queer. This last word is probably the most useful name for it.

Maybe it is a generational thing and easier for young people these days, but back then parents did not really talk to their children about their sexuality – or anyone's, for that matter. As the only son of a single-parent mother and growing up in rural Oudtshoorn, it was particularly difficult for me. Difficult not so much because of the fact that my mother was a church organist at the local Dutch Reformed Church, but because we were good friends and I coveted her approval.

We had been through horror with my father. We developed a predictable solidarity on account of that, and I simply loved her and did not want to disappoint or hurt her. And I still believe that no parent really wants a queer child – my mother's unsurprised sadness when I told her was not on account of any religious moralism or disapproval, but rather because, in her words, a queer life can be 'a lonely life'.

Nonetheless, my great disclosure was accepted with grace and love. My sexuality comes up now and then and even though there is acceptance, 'the conversation' is not something that ever truly ends. One has it again and again: clarifying, explaining, and adapting a kind of eternal explanation that changes in different contexts.

When I got a male partner and introduced him to my mother there was a pause: it is one thing to admit to or be accepting of something in the abstract; being confronted with one's son in bed with another man cannot be very easy. Silence about sexuality is a dubious luxury that straight people take for granted – the thing about being queer and out is that you are necessarily, explicitly wearing your sexuality on your sleeve. You are saying: here I am, I am doing what is unusual and culturally deviant; I am sexual and I am strange.

These dynamics of coming out and living a queer life are, of course, well documented and by now gracefully banal. What is less so is what I call a 'second coming out'. About ten years after I first came out, my mother 'came out' to her friends, her colleagues at the church, and her conservative and oppressive family. She came out not about her own sexuality; rather, she came out about being the mother of a queer son.

This is significant: imagine growing up in the embrace of Dr Verwoerd and his merry men. (I mean this literally: Verwoerd's parents lived in Brandfort, and my mother socialised with the great white liberator often, growing up.) Imagine coming from the rural Free State and being the first in your family to go to university, divorcing and ending up as a music teacher and organist in the Much Deformed Church in a small town – and then taking the conscious decision to tell those close to you that your son is 'other'. I think my mother is a typical contradiction of something queer people take for granted: one comes out to one's parents and then the drama is mostly over. The truth is bigger – coming out is not only about the queer person and their immediate family members. Coming out is also not a one-off event; one does it again, and again, and again.

Parents might choose to keep their children's sexuality under wraps as something never to be spoken of outside the family home. However, if the parent chooses to share the truth about their child's sexuality at the cost of social sanctions to themselves, this opens up a new layer of personal, social complexity.

Of course, my own situation in this regard is suburban and rather soporific. The really interesting parent-child and parent-society dynamics take place in even less accommodating, traditional contexts. Things were difficult for my own mother, but I wonder how much more it may be so in traditional non-middle class and non-vanilla families in townships or in deeply rural South Africa. Do these parents have the luxury of even considering coming out about their children's sexuality? Socially and emotionally, the stress must be compounded exponentially.

However, as the book says, in the end the truth sets you free. Well, not always, but it does help. It gets better.

PHILADELPHIA AND PATRICIDE

My brother and I are both only children. I am an only child, and Ben is an only child. We have the same father, but different mothers; there is an age gap of sixteen years.

I saw Ben quite frequently when he was a small boy, when I visited him, our father, and his mother on weekends when I was a university student. After my relationship with my father broke down completely and I withdrew from him entirely, in early 1994, contact with Ben was one of the things I missed most acutely, and so I was delighted when, at the end of that year, I received a phone call from Ben's mother.

Teresa told me that my father's addictions had spiralled so wildly out of control that she could no longer trust him to drive Ben safely to and then collect him from school. From Penhill – a small, bucolic dirt-road community of bohemian and tree-hugger types on a stretch of road parallel to the N2 highway between Kuils River and Somerset West – the drive to school, in Stellenbosch, was about twenty-three kilometres each way. Teresa's concerns were justified.

At the time I was about to embark on my Master's degree, and I had also received an offer to work as a properly funded research-er for one of my professors. I felt very grown-up, with an office, a lunch break, and a brand new income tax number. Teresa proposed the following: she would drop Ben off at school herself, early in the mornings, and I would collect him after school and drive him home. To make this happen Teresa would take their second vehicle away from my father and give it to me. She would keep the petrol tank full, and after hours and on weekends the car was mine to do with as I pleased. For me this was a splendid prospect: I would have half an hour every school day with Ben, and outside of that my girlfriend Liesl and I would have some freedom of movement. I agreed, and for the next two years this is how my half-sibling and I became better acquainted.

The thing about only children is that we are eerily good at being by ourselves. In order to sustain that, we have vivid inner lives. It was neither easy nor ideal to have a deep and meaningful conversation with a six- or seven-year-old every day, so Ben and I readily slipped into what both of us knew best: fantasy. On Mondays and Wednesdays I had to come up with gruesome and fantastical tales with which to enchant him. On Tuesdays and Thursdays it was his turn to invent and tell me stories. On Fridays we ad-libbed: I would start with a paragraph, and then Ben would contribute a paragraph, and so we would continue until we reached his house. Some days we just chatted. Sometimes we did not talk at all, or we sang strange, invented songs. It was a lovely, lovely time, and I think of those two years with great fondness.

During that time, in 1995 and 1996, Teresa and I stayed in touch mainly via the new wonder of e-mail. We had very little cause to speak face to face, or even on the phone. Our system worked well. However, in early November 1995 my office phone rang, and to my surprise it was Teresa. She needed to see me. It sounded serious. I met her in the parking lot outside the hospital where she had an office. I drove up to where she was parked, got into her car, and for a second or two she just sat there, looking embarrassed.

'Benny's father is having an affair. A woman called Ellen he met at

Lifeline counsellor training. He's also dug up his old gun, his revolver.'

I said nothing.

'I am able to be married to an addict – it's hard, but I know what that entails. But I can't be married to a philanderer. And he's getting more and more violent.'

She turned her face and looked at me as though she was asking my permission for something.

'If there is a gun in this mix, this can't go well. You need to protect Benny. Take it from me.'

I let that hang in the air. I did not care to repeat anecdotes about my inebriated father and guns. At the mention of her son, Teresa nodded. She looked down at her hands.

'You need to get him out, Teresa, and quickly,' I said.

She explained to me that she had already gone to see a lawyer, and he had helped her secure a court order. But unless my father threatened or acted violently towards someone in the presence of witnesses, she was unable to activate the court order and get him out of the house with the help of police. However, if he acted in that way in the presence of witnesses, she would be able to activate the court order and have him removed from her property immediately, on the same day.

We looked straight ahead, at the other cars in the parking lot, as though it was a drive-in cinema. We spoke to each other without looking at one other.

'Well, that's what we need to do, then,' I said.

'What?'

'We need him to threaten or get violent in the presence of witnesses.'

Teresa said nothing.

'I think it's time for a family dinner,' I said.

My father hated his mother. This was understandable. She was the progenitor of her own two dysfunctional children – my father and his sister – and she also begat a pathology that echoes from one generation to the next. I realise on some level that my grandmother, too, must have been the victim of some great-grandparental vice, but in this particular case I am tired of being reasonable, of understanding her pain.

Here was our plan, then: Teresa would get in touch with my and Ben's grandmother and tell her that she desperately needed her down in the Cape for a few days. My grandmother loved to be needed, as it opened people up, like wounds, where she could then burrow and feast like a maggot. My father had had no direct contact with his mother for some years, and would only be informed – by phone – of his mother's arrival about an hour before her plane touched down. During the same phone conversation Teresa would tell him that I too – the estranged son – would be joining them for dinner.

It was our hope that the convergence of all these variables, of all these broken people, would break him further, still. We hoped that the two or so hours between the phone conversation and our choreographed arrival would give my father sufficient time to drug up and drink just enough to be aggressive, but not pass out. We did not tell my grandmother of this plan, and her role in it. Looking back now, and considering that loaded gun, the plan was risky.

Liesl insisted on coming along. Poor Liesl: my sexual ambiguity and ambivalence and my awful family anecdotes fascinated her in the way a fresh car crash or a soap opera fascinate people, and although I did warn her that events might tangle completely beyond anyone's control, she insisted. She told me that she would look after Ben, if anything went south, or if Teresa and I became too involved in events to keep an eye on everyone. I relented, and we (both deeply afraid and deeply exhilarated) drove up to the house as the sun was setting.

Teresa's car was parked in the driveway, which meant that she had already collected my father's mother from the airport. There was no sign of anyone, which meant that everyone was inside. I was worried about the fact that the dogs did not come out to greet us; in my experience dogs only did that when their protective instincts were already engaged elsewhere.

'I have a bad feeling about this,' I told Liesl, who agreed with the sentiment.

I checked that the car doors remained unlocked. I parked the car next to rather than behind Teresa's, so that we could drive past each other or would be able to use either car if we needed to leave in a hurry.

As we got out of the car the front door swung open. Out walked my father, in a T-shirt and shorts. Hair wild, eyes feral, voice loud and half an octave higher than normal. He had lost weight in the nearly two years since I last saw him.

'And here, to render the scene just perfect, ladies and gentlemen,' he boomed, gesticulating towards an unseen audience, 'is arrived our *coup de grâce*: the long-lost son. Oh, how we are playing all the roles.'

My father bowed triumphantly and theatrically showed us the open door. I told Liesl to walk straight past him, fast, and find Ben. My father never looked at her, and backed away slightly, as I came up the stairs to the front door. I was determined not to say one word to him, but I needed to see his eyes, and show him mine.

The next few minutes passed very quickly. The time from this moment until our departure could not have been more than seven minutes. Let me render them as plainly as I can.

I remember the following:

I walk into the lounge and kitchen open-plan area. I note my grandmother and Teresa, both unsmiling and wary, standing in the centre of the kitchen.

I turn to find Ben, who is building something with LEGO. Liesl is kneeling down next to him to help. I bow down to Ben, I go down onto my knees and I turn his face gently towards mine. Ben is crying, softly. I see myself, twenty years earlier, in a different room, and I feel something like anger but much, much older. I feel exceedingly calm. I give Ben a kiss on his cheek and I wipe his silent tears away with my hand, and I swallow before I speak.

'Benny, listen to me now. If anything happens, I will turn and look directly at you and nod my head, like this. If I do that, take Liesl's hand and go straight to my car. Wait for me there. Don't come back to the house.'

My brother smiles at me and nods, returns to the LEGO. I look at Liesl. She nods.

Behind us there is a sound. My father, Teresa, and my grand-mother have disappeared into an adjoining room. Voices are raised but I am unable to make out the words. I stand up, move closer. I wonder where the gun is. My father exclaims something that sounds like a word but is not, and then there is a loud, fleshy crack as my grandmother's head hits the bottom of the door when she falls.

I turn towards Ben, across the room, and nod once. I smile. Ben smiles. He takes Liesl's hand and they walk out the front door.

I need to get Teresa out and we need to leave.

'What are you *doing*?' This is Teresa, shouting. There is fear in her voice. I cannot see what is going on.

My father comes out of the room, fast, and almost walks into me. I look at him. I do not move. He looks at me. I glance into the room and I can see my grandmother, bleeding and confused. It is clear that he struck her, and then she fell. Teresa is bent over her, and is trying to hold something down on the wound, on my grandmother's lower jaw.

I turn to face my father. I consider for an instant that it is interesting to witness someone disintegrate in front of your eyes, as my father lifts up his hands, then lets them drop to his sides. He does not touch me.

'You. I can't touch you,' he says softly.

My father walks away, towards his study. He locks the door behind him. I wonder about the gun again.

I open the bedroom door and say to Teresa, 'We need to go right now.'

'Where's my son?' she says.

'Safe. With Liesl. They're in my car, ready to go.' I bring her her car's keys. 'Can you get her to your car? Can she walk?' I lift my head towards my grandmother. She is standing up, but she seems completely out of it. She is bleeding badly from the cut on her jaw. I feel nothing for her. 'Can she walk?' I say again. 'We need to go right now. The gun.'

This animates the room. Teresa and my grandmother walk out the front door. I turn off the stove and follow them, locking the door behind us. We get into our respective cars.

'Where's Mommy?' Ben asks.

'Right there,' I point her out to him, in the car next to ours. 'She's fine. You can wave at her if you want.'

Teresa waves back at Ben, but her face is turned back towards the house, and the front door.

We make four stops after we leave the house that evening: first, to drop Ben and Liesl at acquaintances, two roads away, to spare Ben the bureaucracy of violence. I am unable to remember the order in which things happened, but we stop at the hospital, where my grandmother is admitted. A social worker comes out to speak to us and Teresa has to intervene and convince her that it was my father, and not me, who perpetrated this mess. My grandmother refuses to make a statement to the social worker and when Teresa asks her if she will support her own statement to the police, my grandmother says, 'Hy is my kind,' refusing, shaking her broken head. I hate her very much right now, but Teresa seems to understand.

We drive to the police station. Teresa shows them the court order. I agree to accompany the police to the house, so that they can remove my father. Teresa joins Liesl and Ben in the safe house, until after my father is taken away.

I go with four policemen to the house. It is dark. The youngest policeman is nervous, and repeats twice 'As 'n fokken hond vir my kom skiet ek hom vrek.'

I get out first, the dogs are outside and I lock them up in the garden shed. The policemen now go into professional mode, and insist that I stay back. They are about to break open the front door when my father opens it. He looks remarkably calm, and sober as a nun. I wait outside. He gathers a few personal items. The most senior policeman appears with my father's gun, which apparently does not have any bullets. We stand outside, politely silent, smoking cigarettes. My father appears and declares that he is ready to leave.

I stay where I am, in a chair on the dark stoep. Once they have gone I will clean up the worst of it before I fetch Teresa and Ben.

The policemen are standing by their two vehicles, waiting for my father as though he is a dignitary rather than a thug. In character, my father turns to me, and speaks the last words to me that I will ever hear him say:

'I know what you did. I can see it now. Paul – fuck you.'

He says this evenly and almost gently, as an afterthought. And he is not my father any more.

Liesl and I only get back to her student house in Stellenbosch about five hours later, in the middle of the night.

Everyone is asleep. I make inane jokes. I say things like 'You can't say I never take you anywhere', or 'I think Christmas at your folks' house rather than mine', until she kisses me to make me stop. She holds my face with both her hands and says that she is so, so sorry. I start to cry. We lie down on her bed. We spoon, with her behind me, holding on to me and whispering to me.

Three days later and it is Monday. I pick Ben up from school. He does not, as he normally would, say 'Hey' to me without looking at me. Instead, he says nothing and carefully puts his backpack on the back-seat. He turns on his seat to look at me, which he does for a long while.

And then he hugs me.

TIME PRESENT

LOST, FOUND, REMAIN

The writer is asleep on the couch in the darkness. It has been light outside for hours, but the blind behind the closed curtains is drawn shut. The room smells unhealthy, of the ashtray on the floor next to the couch – and of something else. There is an empty green wine bottle on its side on the floor towards the side of the room.

The writer does not wake up at the sound of the key in the front door, neither does he stir when his son – the maker of gardens – walks past him to put the paper bag with the groceries on the table. The vegetables still have warm soil on them, and without looking at his father the young man starts to unpack the carrots and potatoes, separating them into two piles.

The gardener walks to the sink and the tap next to the small fridge and rinses his hands. He looks around for a cloth, finds none, then wipes his hands on his trousers. He walks to where the writer is sleeping, picks up the ashtray, empties it into the plastic bag that hangs on a hook below the sink, opens the gas and lights a flame on the stove. He spoons ground coffee into a cloth bag, lowers it into the water in the kettle, and puts it on the flame. Now he turns around to look at the figure on the couch.

Ben does not open the curtains and the blind; he does not want the sudden light to upset the sleeping man. He bends down to get close to the writer's face, for a second he looks at him, and then he says, 'Dad,' touching the sleeping man's shoulder. The writer makes a sound and frowns, but makes no further movement. 'Dad,' the young man says again, and now he pats the old man's shoulder, then holds it and shakes it gently, urgently.

The writer awakes with a fright, draws back his head and inhales quickly, pulls back a fist, horror on his face.

'Dad,' says Ben more loudly, 'it's me.'

The old man exhales, sits up, puts his face in his hands.

'Sorry,' he says. 'Bad dream.'

Ben opens the curtains and blind and the window in the kitchen area on the other side of the room, then he looks for something in the open cupboard.

'Where's the instant oats?'

His father frowns; he is stuffing his pipe where he is sitting on the couch.

'Gave it to Lenie,' he says, then more softly, 'Can't get that shit into my body.'

Ben turns around to look at his father.

'Got to eat something to stabilise your blood sugar in the morning. Otherwise you'll fall again.'

Ben says this matter-of-factly, without irritation. His father says nothing.

'The instant oats takes only two minutes – that was the point.'

When his father still says nothing, Ben turns towards the table, 'Right – fruit and a bun, then.'

The old man drops his matches on the floor, swears, then uses his one hand to feel around his feet for the little box.

'Can't fucking see,' he says.

Ben looks at his father, then says, 'The five-times magnification specs will get here any day now.' The young man checks on the almanac stuck to the wall. 'I ordered them three weeks ago.' He turns back to his father. 'Any day now,' he says again.

'Can't fucking see,' his father says again.

Ben seems to consider something, then says, 'I can ask Teresa about an optometrist at a public clinic?'

The old man shakes his head, smirks. 'Don't bother – your mother won't do anything to help me.'

Ben says nothing; he turns around to pour the coffee.

'Never has, never will,' his father adds.

'I am thinking of getting you a smoothie maker,' says Ben. 'You can use fruit as the basis, but add veggies too – for breakfast.' When his father says nothing, Ben adds, 'That's breakfast covered, and for lunch I can make you sandwiches and drop them off every other day.' Ben looks up, through the kitchen window. 'Every weekend I'll make dinners for your week ahead, and we can keep them in the freezer and you just defrost and eat, in the evenings.'

The old man does not answer. Ben looks around the room, walks over to a desk and a chair in the corner. There are papers and pencil shavings scattered across the surface of the desk, with small piles of books on the floor next to it, and a magnifying glass on top of the books.

'How is work going?' He looks at his father.

'Work,' says the old man, eventually, as if the one word suffices. 'Can't write once it gets dark because I can't fucking see,' he adds.

Ben looks at the lamp on the desk. 'I'll bring a hundred watt and replace the sixty watt one.'

His father shrugs. 'Yes, maybe that'll make me a little less Homeric.'

The writer smiles at his own joke. Ben watches him light the pipe.

'See you tonight, Dad.' Ben has his hand on the door handle. 'Cottage pie for dinner,' he adds.

'What are you up to today?' asks his father, looking up.

The young man hesitates. He seems to consider his options. He breathes in through his nose before he speaks.

'I am meeting Paul for lunch, in Stellenbosch. Then I am coming back here to make your dinner.'

The old man straightens up, slowly, but does not get up from the couch. He turns his head to face his son.

'Paul who?' he asks.

'Paul your son – Paul my brother,' says Ben.

The old man blinks twice but does not speak.

'He contacted me on Facebook last week,' says the young man.

His father is quiet for a few seconds, then he nods. He speaks very softly.

'Why now? Do you know what he wants?'

Ben looks past his father, out the window.

'He says he misses me and he wonders how I am.'

The old man nods again. He looks away from his son.

'How long has it been? Eighteen, twenty years?' He looks back at Ben. The young man considers this.

'I last saw him when I was nine – so, twenty years ago for me,' says Ben. 'Longer for you,' he adds.

Ben watches his father rub the fabric of the couch with his left hand, staring unfocused at the floor, moving his head from side to side. He is thinking, remembering.

'I can hardly remember any of that,' his father says after a while. 'Hardly at all.' The old man closes his eyes and shakes his head slowly as though he is saying no.

'I should be back between five and six,' says Ben. 'Depending on traffic.'

'Son,' says his father, quickly, from the couch. 'Come here.'

The writer holds out his right hand, in Ben's direction. Ben walks towards the old man, takes the outstretched hand and moves down on to his haunches, so his face is at the same level as his father's.

The old man, myopic and unfocused, looks at Ben's face. He moves his hand to his son's cheek, then softly strokes it from the cheekbone to the chin.

'You're my boy,' he says.

Ben holds still; he says nothing. Then he gets up to his full height and walks to the door.

'See you later, Dad.'

'My boy,' the writer whispers, as the door closes. 'My boy.'

* * *

The professor is in the departmental administrator's office, which leads to his own. A well-dressed man in his early sixties appears in the doorway, smiles, apologises for interrupting, and asks after one of the colleagues. It sometimes happens that people drift into the building and walk the corridors in search of people they have heard on a radio programme or seen on the television – or they ask for money. This gentleman appears to be one of the former – harmless enough – so Paul and Magda remain relaxed and polite.

'She's overseas, unfortunately,' Magda informs the visitor.

He tells them that he is a Lategan, from Lategansvlei, not far from Oudtshoorn. Magda and Paul smile at this, explaining that they had, both of them, at various stages of their lives, lived in that town. Mr Lategan is delighted by this news, and enquires after the professor's connection to the town. When Paul tells him that his mother still lives there, Mr Lategan nods and assures the professor that his mother is well known in the community, always so willing to help wherever she can – a real gem. This is good to hear, but given how private, how asocial in many ways the professor's mother is, this does not altogether ring true.

Mr Lategan asks if they can step into the professor's private office, for a quick chat. Magda and Paul glance at each other, but they show him in.

'Don't forget about your meeting,' Magda says, as they have arranged for her to do in such circumstances.

'I'll just be a minute,' Paul tells Magda (and his visitor).

Mr Lategan asks if they can close the door, but Paul tells him that he never does this, for reasons to do with social safety and working with young people. This is not a lie. Often, if one declines a request directly and unapologetically, calmly and with a smile, people accept a 'no' without a fuss.

Paul invites Mr Lategan to sit in the chair on the other side of a coffee table, and then sits down in his usual chair, just able to see Magda's face behind her desk on the far side of the open door. Students do not know this, but this is what Paul always does when he receives anyone but a close personal acquaintance. The result is that he and his visitor are out of earshot from Magda, unless they raise their voices, but Paul is able to attract her attention with a well-aimed look.

'The Lord has led me to you today,' says the visitor. 'When I heard that your mother is a church organist, and that you come from the same town as me . . . It's clear.'

Mr Lategan smiles at the evident truth of what he is saying. Paul waits, no longer smiling, although not antagonistic. When Paul says nothing, the visitor continues.

'I have lost so much in the past two years – and I thank the Lord for that.' He nods to himself, watching the professor. 'It is my own fault,

I know that. The Lord allows our sins to consume us – that's how we learn. And He is merciful.'

He looks at Paul; Paul looks at him.

'What can I do for you, Mr Lategan?' Paul says, softly but formally.

The visitor realises that he needs to speed up.

'I am an alcoholic. I have lost everything because of the bottle. But I'm determined to get well, to make it up to my family. I'm about to be admitted to the rehab clinic at Klapmuts.'

He looks at the professor, but Paul does not move. Paul is good at this; he waits five seconds.

'Mr Lategan,' Paul starts again, making a point to be slightly formal, but ostensibly respectful. 'This is an academic department at a university. I'm not sure what I can do for you. And I do have that meeting I need to get to.'

The visitor knows this is the endgame: now or never.

'I need three hundred rand to check in, at the clinic.' He leaves it at that. Mr Lategan is not so bad at this himself. They look at each other.

'We don't keep money in the office. And I certainly do not have hundreds of rands in my wallet.'

Mr Lategan is prepared for this. 'Maybe you could draw the money,' he suggests helpfully, 'or just give me what you can?' He does not sound unreasonable. It is almost as if he is not begging.

'Mr Lategan,' Paul says after taking a breath and exhaling, 'I am not going to draw any money. I do not want to give you any money. I am not going to give you any money.'

After that they say nothing. They do not break eye contact. There is no aggression in the room. There is nothing more to say. Paul gets up without hurrying, as does Mr Lategan, and they take the few steps towards the door, which Paul opens wide. Mr Lategan leaves without saying another word.

Paul takes out his phone and posts a message on the departmental WhatsApp group: 'Well-dressed mature gentleman in corridor. Alcoholic. Asking for money. Does not seem dangerous but watch out if he asks for a chat.'

He turns towards Magda, who is just then reading the message on her own phone. She looks up.

'Jesus, did he misjudge his audience,' Paul says. Magda smiles.

'Right, I'm going out to lunch.' He locks his office door and turns around to face her.

'Same place as usual?' she asks, keeping her eyes on her computer screen.

'Yes.' He hesitates. 'I've put in leave for the rest of the day. So I'll see you tomorrow.'

Magda stops and lifts her face to look at him. Paul is a creature of habit; he does not vary his routine. This is unusual.

'Are you meeting a secret someone?' She smiles at him and puts the stem of her glasses between her teeth, widens her eyes dramatically, teasing him. Paul can tell she is genuinely curious.

'Oh, you know me,' he says. He winks at her and walks out into the corridor.

'Have fun,' she says behind him. He can hear that she is smiling.

Paul wonders about that little exchange. He could simply have said that he was leaving for the day, and she would have let him be. Why the over-explanation? Why did he talk about lunch, and the restaurant? He is slightly irritated – surprised, rather – with himself. The fucking alcoholic has unsettled him. Today of all days.

Paul prefers not to be noticed. He has always been good at managing the various parts of his life, keeping them discrete. He is surprised at his anticipation of this meeting, of the prospect of this afternoon. He feels very alive.

In order to elude others in the corridor, he takes the closest flight of stairs, walks down one floor, and then towards the lifts. He wants to get to the restaurant early – at least fifteen minutes – so that he can select a seat, get settled, and observe his half-brother's approach.

* * *

At 12:57 on a Tuesday in the early autumn, the writer finally abandons any pretence of work and opens a fresh bottle. Forty-four kilometres away, the gardener is in his bakkie, approaching the parking area opposite the restaurant where he will meet his brother after a twenty-year absence. The professor sits at a restaurant table, watching the entrance, waiting, waiting.

It occurs to Paul that he may not recognise Ben when he walks through the door. He discards the idea – surely he'll know his own brother. At that moment a white bakkie drives past, outside in the street, and he thinks he recognises the driver. Paul realises that the face that he glimpsed – fleetingly, from the side – is his own.

When Ben appears in the doorway, Paul smiles and gets up. Ben sees him and recognises a younger version of his father. The brothers lift their hands and give each other a wave. When they are in front of each other, their eyes are at the same level, and have the same colour.

'Brother,' says Paul.

'Hello, Paul,' says Ben.

They smile – when they do this, both of their upper lips bend slightly upwards towards the right – and after a second, they embrace.

They order sparkling water. The conversation is easy. The details are not important. To someone at a nearby table, it might look as though they have known each other all their lives. The physical resemblance is clear – father and son, maybe. They talk quietly, private-

183

ly, and now and then there is a laugh. Now and then there is a moment of silence, but it is relaxed, unforced.

To each other, they provide quick chronologies of their own lives. There is not much time, so they editorialise as little as possible, sticking to the facts. They have a lot of ground to cover. To save time, to keep it light, they switch to a question-and-answer format.

Paul: Do you believe in God?

Ben (smiles): God, no.

Paul: What do you do to satisfy your metaphysical itch, to make meaning?

Ben: I meditate.

Paul: Buddhism?

Ben: Yes.

Paul: Have you travelled to India, Nepal, Bhutan?

Ben: Wrong kind of Buddhism – I am interested in the kind they practise in South Korea, Japan.

Paul: What music do you like?

Ben: The minimalists. Tavener, Pärt – that kind of thing.

Paul smiles. 'Me too. And Swedish and Norwegian electronic stuff.'

'Of course,' Ben smiles.

Paul: What books do you read?

Ben: Non-fiction, mostly. Some poetry. The French Romantics. Rimbaud.

Paul: Whom do you sleep with?

Ben: No one. It does not interest me.

Paul: And if you had to?

Ben: I do not have to.

They play this game for a while. It's fun; it's useful. Paul leads and Ben follows. They access important information, somehow without becoming intrusive or too deep.

They switch from water to cappuccinos, and as they wait for the coffee, Paul says 'Can we talk about him quickly – get it out of the way?'

'Sure,' says Ben.

'All I want to say is that I don't want you to feel compromised. I'm not interested in contact with . . . Dad.'

When Paul says the word, he stops.

'My God,' he continues, 'I just realised that only you and I can call him that.'

Ben nods.

Paul goes on: 'I am not interested in you because I want to get access to him – I'm interested in *you*, Ben; I want to get to know *you*. We can talk as much or as little about him as makes you comfortable, but I'm not particularly interested in him.'

Ben nods again. He looks at Paul. 'I think you saw the worst of him, all those years ago. I was so little when everything blew up.' Ben seems to have stopped, but then he continues. 'When I got depression – really bad, debilitating – in my early teens, and in the years that followed, he was so good to me. He was the one who stuck with me and cared for me, when for years I was unable to leave my bed, and the house. He helped me get through school, to finish my studies afterwards, to get up and enter life.' Ben is facing Paul, but it seems to his brother as though he is looking right through him, at a point behind his head. 'I thank the universe for him.' Before Paul can respond, Ben adds, 'He drinks, he gets along with no one, he blames everyone else, he has only me in the world.'

Paul regards his brother. Ben says nothing more.

'I think you're right,' says Paul. 'I did see the worst of him – but maybe also the best, when he was a young man. But the weight of history . . .' Paul shrugs.

Ben looks away.

After a few seconds, Paul says, 'I sometimes wonder how I may have been different, how things may have turned out differently, if he and I had a better, less extreme history.' Paul takes a sip of his cappuccino, he remembers something. 'I think all of it has made me something that I wouldn't otherwise have been – and that's good and bad, I guess. But it's also made me hard in ways that are unattractive.' When Ben says nothing, Paul continues. 'Earlier today an alcoholic showed up at my office and asked for money. I said no, and he left. Maybe, if I were a kinder man, I would have felt empathy for him. But I don't. And I don't want to. I am enraged. Which means that I'm failing. Because what I want to feel is nothing.'

Ben says nothing. He shifts his body closer to the table, watching his brother.

Paul goes on. 'You know, on my drive home, to Wellington, every day on the left-hand side of the road I go past an abandoned dilapidated little house. It used to be one of those worker's houses that Boland painters so often romanticise. The door and window have been bricked up, I think to make the house into something else, to fit it to a new purpose. Maybe it is a barn now, with an opening on the other side. Or maybe it's been bricked up to keep people from using it as a place to sleep. The building that used to be a house is now no longer what it was when it started its life. Its ideal type has been changed, destroyed. As a lodging, it has become inauthentic. What it had been originally has been changed to make room for something else, but traces of the original remain.'

Paul pauses, then he goes on. 'I went to see a psychologist when I was twenty years old. Her name was Sarah. I told her that my main problem was a sense of inauthenticity. The experiences I'd had growing up had turned me into something I wasn't supposed to be.

Yes, traces of the real me remained, but my door and my window had been bricked up, and I am become . . . something else. Apparently such feelings are fairly typical for people like us. That psychologist spent over two years helping me tolerate and then learn to love what I'd become. She convinced me that there is no ideal journey. But what if, hey, Benny? If Dad loved me, and if I loved him, would I have been gentler towards that drunk, this morning? If Dad and my mom loved each other, would I have been a more authentic version of myself? If my girlfriend at university and I were not so meticulous about birth control, would I have been a good father? If the person I was in love with did not leave because he had to run from himself, would we have been happy now, living together? Was that my ideal relationship, foiled? What am I asking? What is it I want? Is my life inauthentic? I guess I don't really think so. But I consider the possibilities of a more vanilla existence – those sister selves – and I do wonder.'

Ben nods, but says nothing. Paul smiles, he feels self-conscious.

'But I've got to work on being kinder,' says Paul. 'Maybe I should have given that man the money he wanted. Or rather, maybe I should not have given him the money, but for the right reasons. I should have thought of him, rather than of myself. I should not have enjoyed his humiliation quite as much.' Paul takes a sip of his cappuccino. 'But think of the skins I'd have to shed, eh?' he smiles.

'I think this is the most significant thing to have happened in my life,' says Ben, and when he sees that Paul is not sure what he is referring to, he clarifies, 'This,' motioning with his hand, pointing at Paul and then at himself, 'getting to know you again. For years . . . I was so out of it, unable to get up from the couch, with my back to the room. I would not have been able to do this two years ago or maybe even one year ago.' Ben considers something for a second, then he nods to himself and says, 'Ja, I think this is the most significant thing to have happened to me since I have started to re-emerge into the world.'

Ben looks at his watch. 'I need to go. I need to cook Dad dinner tonight. He is not eating right and I am worried about his sugar levels. He drinks too much sherry.'

Paul says nothing.

They leave the restaurant. Outside, they hug goodbye.

'Listen,' says Paul, 'can we please do this regularly? Can we please be in each other's lives now, brother?'

Ben nods yes. 'I would like that very much.' He smiles at Paul. 'Let us remain.'

THE SEER'S TOWER

Memory is identity. As aphorisms go, this is a good one. It is certainly more charming than 'The child is father to the man', or 'Character is destiny', which both augur dark and inescapable futures, hopelessness. Also, I have come to view memory as a uniquely mutable thing: the older I get, the greater my faith, my hope is in the ability to transform, reclaim, and rehabilitate the past. And if I can change memory, then I can change identity. I find this hopeful, optimistic. That said, memorial mutability could go the other way, too, towards depressive insights and the shattering of some helpful denial or friendly ignorance. But still.

I considered all of this driving back from a third meeting of the Philadelphic Society – Ben and my secret brotherhood – in which we participate exclusively, not inviting along our parents, or our friends. We have agreed to get together in cafés and restaurants, or in open green spaces; it does not occur to us to host each other in either of our homes – that would be too propulsive into some kind of unready familiarity. Somehow, seeing each other in spaces where we have to focus on each other, neutrality and anonymity around us, renders our meetings more intimate.

My reacquaintance with my half-brother had been unplanned. I was having dinner with two friends of mine – a philosopher and a therapist – and we were swopping anecdotes and bits of family history. I told them that I miss my brother and that, when he was a very small boy, we used to be quite close. But life got in the way and we have not seen each other or spoken in many years.

My therapist friend asked me how old this man was. She had done it on purpose, of course, I caught her 'this man' immediately, and I told her that Ben was now almost thirty.

'He's old enough so you can contact him without parental consent or involvement, you know,' she pointed out. 'You can just send him a message via e-mail or Facebook.'

'Ha,' I said, and put my fork down on the plate. I stared at my friends, processing this evident, obvious truth. He's an adult; he's not a child.

'You know, Paul,' my philosopher friend said, 'for someone as self-aware as you, you can be pretty un-self-aware.' We laughed at this, together, I agreed with the statement, and I told my friends that I would think about it.

Late that evening, I found my brother on Facebook. Without thinking about it for too long, resisting the instinct to avoid, I sent the following private message:

Dear brother!

It has been so long since we've been in contact. I think of you often and I miss you. Would it be okay with you if we get back in contact with each other? How are you?

All the best from
Big Brother

The next morning, this waited for me:

Howzit Paul

What a cool surprise to hear from you, it indeed has been a while! Are you in SA? If so maybe we can grab a coffee sometime? There's a hell of a lot to chat about since last we talked.

In any case, hope you have been keeping well over the years. Chat soonest ;)

Warm regards
B.

A number of surprises have emerged, in retrospect, from meetings of the Philadelphic Society: (1) We are kind, we are gentle with each other. It is as though we have both emerged from the past tender and pink, we are fragile and without skins, softly, softly caring for each other, careful not to cause any pain; (2) We have lost many years, so we spend no time on small talk; (3) We are remarkably focused on discussing what matters, and we do so truthfully, honestly, including questions such as: How do you express yourself creatively? What makes you angry? What makes you happy? What do you do to combat darkness, depression? And so on. Not that we spend the time all Meaningful and Heavy: there is much laughter and irreverence.

The other remarkable thing is our similarities: physically, we are exactly the same height, we have the same teeth, the same eyes, but we also share oddly similar mannerisms and tastes: our habit of touching our foreheads; how we push the hair out of our eyes; our subtle but noticeable (if you look for it) way of pulling our clothes away from our bodies; the way we use the word 'delicious', as a moral judgement; we both love cats; we both have a very slight lisp, when we are not speaking consciously; and – most gratifyingly – we both love the music of Arvo Pärt. Some of this I can understand – we have in common a significant chunk of genome, after all – but much of this remains rather mysterious to both of us, only children that we are.

The one thing we do not have in common, though, is a private sense of safety around our father. To me, our common progenitor is my father; to Ben, he is Dad. And still, I love the sense of wonder – the cosy kinship – I feel when he speaks of 'Dad', with such facility, and the fact that only I have the right to do the same, referring to the same man. I always thought that, if someone were to give me an opportunity to ask one question of Ben's dad, of my father, then I would ask him how he can stand being who he is, and not kill himself.

Ben's dad is not well. He does not take good care of himself, physically, and recently Ben and I touched on the reality that he may not be available to Ben for many years more. Previously, I would have been indifferent to my father's life expectancy. But that evening, after my first meeting with Ben, as grown-ups, unusually I found myself hoping Dad will be around for a bit longer – for Ben. Ben's dad is good for him, and good to him. Or so Ben says.

I remember when I, as a teenager and then at university, up until the collapse of our relationship, feigned indifference to the world of words and books and literature. This was my father's world, this was the thing he cherished most, and so I needed to put a wall of ice between that and me. I would look away or physically move away from my father's bookshelves, whenever he was near. Or I would affect apathy about a beautiful passage my father read out loud, needing to hide the fact that actually the words had given me goose bumps, that the beauty of those words rendered me quite sad or speechless. 'Yes, very pretty,' I would say, and look away.

Now my father – Ben's dad – is a man of very limited means, un-well, and being cared for by his son, by the one who loves him and trusts him. Two quotations came to me, as I considered all of this: 'I've been to every single book I know, to soothe the thoughts that plague me so.' This is from a song by Sting, and when I sang it, un-thinkingly, in my father's presence, once, he said to me 'Yes, I know the feeling.'

I also recall another line, from a song by Sufjan Stevens which Ben knows, that we recently discussed: 'Oh my mother, she betrayed us, but my father, loved and bathed us.' Yes, I wish him good health and a few more years yet, because Ben loves him, and I love Ben.

After my meeting with my brother I took the last turn off the N1, heading towards Wellington. I wondered whether Ben's dad, my fa-ther, still has access to books. He has no money, he is not well, so is he able to buy them, or to get to a library? I hope that he does, that he is able to. To soothe the thoughts that plague him so.

WOMEN'S DAY

My brother and I have fallen into the habit of meeting up on or near public holidays. We met at the end of March not quite on Human Rights Day, but close; then around Freedom Day, in April; then on Workers' Day, in May; most recently on the Sunday after Youth Day, in June. We will meet again on Women's Day. All of this is pure coincidence, but I like the ritualistic regularity; it is as though we are on some kind of significant, meaningful schedule. Maybe we will arrange something for Heritage Day, near my birthday towards the end of September.

When we last met it also happened to be Father's Day, which means different things for Ben and for me; at the end of our lunch and our conversation my brother announced that he needed to go, to prepare his dad's dinner, to mark the occasion. Afterwards, when I told my mother about our meeting, she asked whether I went along with Ben, to see my father. I laughed at her joke, but she was serious; my mother, after all she has been through, remains so much more forgiving than me. I told her no, that I have no desire to see Ben's dad, my father, because of reasons that should be obvious. My new relationship with Ben has not changed that. In fact, I told her, Ben and I spend little time discussing his dad, my father. That much is true.

My reacquaintance with my brother has kicked up a lot of mud.

All my life I have craved and romanticised a serene and quiet emotional field; I want my inner and emotional life as calm as the Dead Sea floor. But now I am starting to loosen up. And although I mostly appreciate the richness and sympathy that this has enabled, there are areas of my emotional field that move off the reservation. After my meetings with Ben, I often feel exhilarated, energised, sated, but also vaguely disturbed, discomfited, distressed. I sometimes feel these things all at the same time, and then I become conflicted, oscillating between feeling giddy and weepy. But I go with this, I channel it and I process it; I am not helpless; I have resources; I am an adult.

Sometimes, though, a little debris from the past slips through, activating elements deeply hidden in the lizard part of my mind. It takes a while to name them and own them. It is hard. Sometimes resolution is not easy, or remains elusive.

So here's one: recently I asked Ben whether he has told his dad about our meetings, about his sons having re-established contact. My brother answered in the affirmative, saying that he has mentioned it. I could not resist the next question, although every instinct towards that calm sea floor pulled me in the other direction. I asked Ben what his dad said to this. Ben told me two things: (1) My father asked my brother how I am, and Ben then told him that I am doing well; (2) My father reflected in silence for a few seconds, and said something that entered and exited me at great speed, and at great volume, like neutrinos, which are abundant, everywhere, and quite invisible.

I have to concentrate now, because my mind has filtered Ben's account into something that I protect myself against with such profound, quiet energy that recounting it accurately is beyond me. I am unable to recall the words, but what my brother told me was that – and here I paraphrase – his dad said that when he thinks about that time in his life, when I was in it, he can just shake his head, and be grateful that he is beyond it. Ben told me (without using these words, but the meaning was clear) that his dad does not want contact with me.

At this point I need to explain something. When I ceased contact with my father in February 1994, it was an act of power, or, at least, of taking power, of self-protection. Part of that power was and remains situated in the premise that I can control my father's contact with and access to me. Over the years there have been a few (not many – two in total, beyond 1994) approaches from my father. I shunned those approaches. There was tacit power and satisfaction in knowing that my father wanted to contact me, but that I said no, I declined, I took that control and celebrated it within myself.

But the truth is my father does not want contact with me. He has taken note of the fact that his other son does have contact with me, but he will not pursue that himself.

The way Ben explained it (briefly, and I did not seek further clarification), was that his dad would experience such contact as too painful, that he (Ben's dad) would be reminded of too many things from the past that should now remain there. Ben's dad did not blame me for anything, but it was a different time, a dark time, and Ben's dad is now a different person. He cares for Ben and Ben cares for him. He is flawed, and the darkness of those years is something that came from him, but he cannot or will not pick up those lines of existence.

Ben delivered this message delicately. My brother and I understand unspoken fragilities and rawness between us. He did not want to hurt me. My brother is a gentle and a shy man, incapable of lying, and I think the delivery of such a message must have been hard for him.

It took many days for me to go back to that moment, after our previous meeting. I meet with Ben not because he is my father's son, or because he and I are our father's sons, but because I am genuinely interested in him. We do not usually discuss the past, or our parents. We discuss what is going on in our lives now, and we are getting to know each other as individuals. We both struggle with a proclivity for disassociation, and we revere our conversations as moments of supreme immediacy and reality.

And yet.

I find myself today not quite ready to express fully what I tried to do (incompletely, imperfectly) above, because it means I have to acknowledge the fact that I am hurt. And behind the hurt lies feelings that I have fought so very hard to foreswear, deny, banish. Daddy issues are so unattractive, slightly embarrassing and, frankly, boring in a middle-aged man.

And so here we are on the day before Women's Day. This morning I drove my mother to the ophthalmologist, for a check-up one month after her eye operation. She's fine, all is well. We drive back from Somerset West, and my music collection is on random selection on the car's sound system. The song is well advanced before it dawns on me that I need to switch off the music. It is Tori Amos's song 'China'. I wake up to this when my mother points out that she has never heard this, it's good, who's the artist. With my mouth I tell her about Amos, and her music, which as a music teacher my mother appreciates, she says something about harmony, but in my mind I'm not listening because I know precisely why I never play this in my mother's presence: late in the song Amos modulates, there's a wordless segment where she changes the rhythm and wails – six notes only – but I know those sounds are so much like moments in the music of Kate Bush that my mother won't miss it. In the 1970s my father was really into Kate Bush, he played her incessantly, and at that time he was fucking Vivienne, in Bloemfontein. This was a very unhappy time for my mother, and to this day – although she recognises Kate Bush's musical mastery – my mother cannot stand her. I have been at pains to keep such instances of pain from my mother, and so I freeze, behind the wheel of the car, and I think of strategies to end the song, but my mother is listening actively.

Then those six notes come, the modulation washes over us, and I wait. My mother turns her head and looks over the lush green fields and the sprinkling of snow on the mountains, and she says 'Baie soos Kate Bush.' She says no more, I wait for the song to end, and then mercifully the music system shuffles to something else. My mother is quiet for maybe half a minute, and then points out something in the distance. The moment has passed.

My mind drifts towards my meeting with Ben, and my father's statement about not wanting contact with me. I think about the Tori Amos song, where it took us, I think about the debris that we carry within us, and I allow feeling to get kicked up, inside me. But the thing about feelings is that, when you allow them, it is hard to curate which ones arrive and which ones do not. Yes, there is joy in feeling, but there is also its photo negative. I am not sure what to do with that.

An hour later my mother asks me what I am going to do on Women's Day. I tell her I'll be meeting my brother in Franschhoek, for lunch. This pleases her. She suggests again that I should invite Ben to dinner, to a braai; she'll cook for us, she'll stay out of the way; it'll be fun to have him see where I live. I tell her again that my brother is a shy man, and leave it at that. I think my mother thinks that I am ashamed of her, but the truth is that I do not want her to experience something like that moment in the car, and be reminded of Kate Bush, of infidelity and of violence. I need to protect her. There would be too many feelings in play, too many identities active. Brother. Son. Her son. His sons. No – too hard.

My mood is dark and I consider telling my brother about his dad's more extreme behaviour. About how, when I was eleven years old, a year after fleeing my father's violence, he follows us to Oudtshoorn. My mother has a nervous breakdown (not rhetorically; this is clinically diagnosed), and my father drives her to George, across the mountain, for weekly sessions with a psychiatrist. The doctor prescribes sleep therapy. My father administers this at home. But while I am at school and my mother is supposed to sleep, my father gives her the medication, then keeps her awake. As in Bloemfontein, she has to stand erect on a table, naked, for hours, while he takes various aspects of her personality, her life, and destroys them. Her parents, her choices, her appearance, her morals, her identity as mother, her identity as wife. He takes each of them and over the course of weeks he takes his time, keeps her awake, keeps her standing for hours upon hours upon hours, and slowly, calmly talks her into denying it all. He breaks her. He nearly kills her. We very nearly do not escape. To this day we bleed a little.

I want to point out to Ben that his dad did this not when he was drunk – not all the time – and I want the uncomfortable truth about his dad being a monster to trickle into him.

I want to print out every single thing I have exposed about my father, and send it to Ben's dad, with a bottle of wine, and a card to congratulate him on the fact that he has been able not to kill himself.

I want to eviscerate every single wife beater, philanderer, violent male in the world. I find myself this afternoon at Mugg & Bean in a shopping centre, after our visit to the specialist, listening to a husband administer a petty cruelty to his wife, at a nearby table, and I catch myself fantasising about ways to hurt him.

I want to burn down the school where my mother worked, which refused to make her appointment permanent because of her breakdown.

I want to castrate the school principal who refused to defend her appeal to be paid the same as her male colleagues, because as a female she was 'not the breadwinner'.

I want to slit the throat of the medical aid administrators who refused her medical aid, when I entered high school, because of her mental illness.

I want to spit in the face of the God to whom my mother prayed, because He allowed all of this.

To my father, I want to say:

Shame on you.

Fuck you.

I love you.

CONNECTION

My brother is very polite. Ten minutes before the appointed time when we were supposed to meet for lunch, he sends me a voice message.

'Hello Paul, I am running a bit late. There was a stop-go on the R44 that delayed me. I'll be between ten and fifteen minutes late.'

Ben speaks in beautiful, complete sentences. Apparently contractions (like that 'I'll', in his voice note) are rare in his diction. When he arrives, as he approaches, he gives a little wave, from side to side, from just above his waist.

'Sorry I am late.'

I tell him it's fine, that it gave me time to read to the end of the chapter of my book, and to study the menu.

Ben never wants to eat anything. We have fallen into a routine: I arrive first, I watch the door for his approach, he arrives, we hug (I initiate), the menus come, he does not want to eat, I order something we can share, the food arrives, I cut the food into small pieces, and then we both pick at it while we talk. At first he does this haltingly, for my sake, to be polite, but eventually he forgets about not wanting food and eats heartily, talking while he picks up the pieces with his fingers, chews, swallows. This is how we have been doing it now for months.

Prior to our meeting I asked Ben to send me something he had written. He hesitated, and so I pestered him on WhatsApp, remind-ed, pushed, asked for it again. And so he had sent me something – a prose poem.

'What's your process?' I ask him.

'Oh, with that one I just free-associated, right after I woke up in the morning.'

'Do you plan or have a theme ahead of time, before you start to write?' I ask.

He looks surprised, as though such a notion is exotic. He shakes his head no. He does not ask me the same question, but I tell him anyway. I tell him that I do the work in my car, in my head, while I am on my commute to and from work. I switch off the sound system and over time – hours, days – I wait for something to emerge, to scratch. I allow it to just be, I try not to overthink it. What starts out as a suspicion, as something intuited, eventually turns into a small stone in my shoe: it will irritate me until I express it. But I do not plan it. Eventually I sit down and I just play with it. The only thing I want to transmit, or capture, is a feeling, a sense, rather than any specific narrative or trajectory.

My brother nods. 'A feeling. Yes.'

He continues: 'There is no beginning and no end to it. When I write something, it feels as though I am expressing something forever in the present.'

I want to comment on this, but something tells me to keep quiet. Ben is looking past me, thinking.

'I write to move back into myself, rather than to express something outward.' I remain quiet for a bit longer, but I can tell my brother is done. He looks back directly at me.

I tell my brother that this last comment of his, about his writing to reach inwards, towards himself, is interesting; it sounds as though he does this to connect with himself. I tell him that the purpose of my own bits of writing is to reach outwards, to connect to something outside. He considers this, nods. I tell Ben that this pleases me, this notion that one can perform the same activity but for what feels to me like opposite motivations. When I say this Ben goes quiet. My brother is in a serious mood today, and I worry that I may have overstepped.

'This is not oppositional at all,' he says at last. He is quiet for a few seconds and then he goes on. 'I do this to connect with myself; you do this to connect with something outside of yourself.' Ben takes a breath, and continues. 'But the activity, the aspiration is the same: we do this to *connect*.'

My brother sits back. I can see that he is tired. Ben has trouble remembering anything specific prior to his re-emergence into the world; he wants to reconnect with himself. It is as though he is an inside or underwater creature experimenting with the outside, as though he has recently emerged from the water, and his skin is not yet formed. He is from a different place, fragile; one has to be gentle, take it slow.

Every time we meet, both of us grow weary after about two hours in each other's company. It is still not as though we only ever discuss things that are heavy and serious – on the contrary: we are meticulous about keeping things even and light.

'What do you remember?' I ask him.

He shakes his head. 'I remember nothing.' I wait for him to go on. 'I remember images, but they feel second-hand, derivative, like a dream of a dream.' I remain quiet. 'If I think about these things they come alive, move out of focus, I lose them.'

Ben shakes his head, he picks up his glass of water and slices of lemon. I realise that I have exhausted him; I shall make no more demands today; I need to talk; he needs to rest.

'Do you want to know what I remember?' I ask. He looks up, waits. 'I remember our first meeting. You were three months old and I was sixteen, I'd just arrived for a term-break holiday, with Dad and your mom. I picked you up and Dad told me to watch your neck, to support your head, and as I turned around I smiled, your head lolling on my arm, unfocused, and then Dad took a photograph of us. I have it still, that photograph.'

I go on. 'I remember the night you were born. Saturday night, 28 January 1989. It was warm and I was watching the movie *Firestarter* on television. The phone rang and I ran for it, I'd been waiting for news the whole day. It was Dad, telling me I have a brother.'

Ben needs very little from me. He never asks me questions; his demands on me are slight and benign. I consider a question. It is about our father.

'Do you want to know what's my best memory of Dad?' I ask. He nods. I regret the question immediately, and for a moment I panic, because I do not remember anything. But I know this is not true – the thing about our father is that, in amongst all the horror of his humanity, there are specs of incredible beauty, and strange grace.

'My best memory of our father,' I tell my brother, 'is a cold morning in early 1991, when I was eighteen years old. I was waiting for a train, at Blackheath station, to take me to Stellenbosch. Dad had just dropped me off a few minutes earlier, and I was standing on the platform, watching damp breath, smelling the metal from the tracks. And then I felt myself being observed, and turned my head, and there he was, smiling at me from a short distance away. And I smiled back at him. And for what felt like the first time ever we stood smiling at each other, simply man and boy, father and son, without the interference of distrust, or fear, or the need for artifice. He'd turned the bakkie around, came back to drive me to Stellenbosch himself, but first he'd take me to a breakfast of toast and Ricoffy at the Springbok Café.'

'That sounds like a good day,' Ben says.

'It was,' I say.

'Connection,' says Ben.

METAPHYSICS

When I was six years old my father and I took a drive to buy fish and chips. He told me about creation, and that there used to be a time when time did not exist. I told him that the very notion was absurd. So when did it start, he asked, and I said it started when God made it. There was silence and I asked who made God, and my father smiled and said that one needs to know the mind of God to know that answer.

When I was eleven years old my father made some fine point about Thomas Merton's mystical Christianity, and I asked him what it would mean for all his books – all his books on religion, on Christ – if Christ never existed. My father seemed unconcerned and said that the question was irrelevant: Christianity does not require Christ.

When I was twenty years old I went running with my father, every weekend. He was living in a wild, verdant place, and he was constructing a garden in monastic shapes; he was making leaded glass windows, and pointed out how the light in medieval cathedrals signified the presence of God, via the stained glass; he was rewriting the Psalms as rhyming quatrains, to chant as he ran, as monks do in Eastern religions. My father told me that Christ does not need Christianity.

Last Sunday my brother explained to me the differences between the various kinds of Buddhism, as I was chasing a green olive on my plate with a fork.

DEBRIS

I wake up. Was I asleep? I tell myself this was a dream, but I know it is a memory.

This was many years ago. Ben must have been, what, seventeen years old. His mother phoned me and said he needed a positive male role model.

'And you phoned me,' I laughed. She said nothing. 'Of course,' I said seriously. She mentioned a diagnosis. She feels helpless. I understand this, and nod as I adjust the phone.

'All you need to do,' she says, 'is to reach out to him. E-mails, a phone call now and then.'

I understand. 'Of course,' I say again, nodding.

A friend, over dinner that evening, remarks that I seem quite affected – quite upset – by the request. A little debris from the past; an atavistic excitement, which poisons as much as it arouses. I need to proceed carefully.

And so I phone once a week, then once every two weeks, then once a month. The conversations are brief and contrived. I send books I think he would enjoy. Our e-mails are perfunctory. I try to be warm, fraternal, to let down my guard, but the consistency belongs to the teenager: supreme politeness, reflections on each of my comments, but no news of his own in return. I am not sure I can keep this up.

We do this for months (nearly a year), but then I buckle. Contact becomes sporadic, then it falls away. There is no further appeal from the teenager, or from his mother.

I remember all of this, half-asleep, a few nights ago. The reality of this, and of this memory, wakes me up completely. I had remembered this all wrong: contact did not just wane, I ended it. I abandoned him.

But now it is re-established, and I have to remain patient. I must not allow myself to get in the way. I need to calibrate, moderate my expectations. I have friends who help me do this, they encourage contact, they remind me how this works.

At dinner, though, I nod at my friends' suggestions, but in my mind I shake my head; I don't know if this can work. I wish just once he'd ask me how I am.

FUNNY HA-HA

I tell a friend how funny my father was. Or is.

'Funny fucked-up, or funny ha-ha?' she asks.

'Funny ha-ha,' I say.

She shakes her head and asks for an example. I am frustrated to find that nothing jumps to mind. I am concerned that my accounts, my anecdotes, have rendered my father a monster. And a monster he was – is – for sure. But not only that. And that is the point, surely. For it was the juxtaposition with the bright side that rendered the darkness so complete.

I am unable to remember, and this makes me smile, embarrassed. I yawn and look away, as I do in such circumstances. But for the rest of the day it gnaws at me. Not insistently; I have to remind myself to think of it. But think of it I do.

'Oh yes!' I say to myself, in my car, later that same day. I am by myself, driving fast, but at the memory I laugh out loud.

My father once answered a knock at the door, sauntered over, in his hand a glass containing a clear liquid, he opened the door wide, and smiled at the man and the woman. He looked them over: suits, a briefcase, neat haircuts, shiny shoes, pamphlets at the ready.

'Hang on,' he said, a finger to his lips, when one inhaled to speak. 'You're Jehovah's Witnesses, aren't you?'

They exchanged glances, smiled at him, and answered in the affirmative. He took a swig of the liquid into his mouth, tasted the raisin undertones, enjoyed the effect of it in his nose, at the back of his throat, and exhaled on them.

'Well, it's your lucky day,' he said to them. 'For I am Jehovah. How are we doing?'

I laugh. I am driving much more slowly now. I've had a memory, so I can relax. Now that I am remembering – at last, after years of white noise – any reluctance of memories makes me feel lonely and disconnected. I look out the window and will another one.

The phone rang. My father put the glass down, walked over to the phone stand.

'Trevor!' someone boomed from the receiver. (Clearly a wrong number – there were no Trevors there.)

'Yes,' my father shouted back into the phone, 'let's fuck!' My father put the phone down, winked at me, picked up his glass, and returned to his pipe, and to his book.

I make myself think of another. I feel the sink, the drop into some other place, like a drug.

My father was dropping me off at the bus stop. I was at school and my father had brought me to the bus stop to go back home after a holiday. My father shone like a sun on those in his presence, when he was well, when he was present, when he was friendly. This close to the ritual separation, we could both relax, because the days behind us were over, and we were able to return to our lives. There was now no expectation to honour, no pattern to fear, no role to satisfy. And so my father talked about this and that. He pointed out the luggage sorter: a burly man about my father's age, the Intercape uniform just slightly too small, wrinkled.

'Watch this,' said my father. He walked over to the man. 'Hello,' he said, 'didn't we play rugby together? Team of sixty-five, matric, Malmesbury?'

The man beamed. 'Yes,' he said. 'Yes to the rugby,' he qualifies, 'but team of sixty-seven. Parow High.'

'Ah,' said my father, 'I thought you looked familiar. I'm sure we ran into each other at some stage.' My father gave the man a cigarette. They looked up at the sky and talked about the weather.

'You see,' said my father when he got back to me. 'I don't know that man at all. He's from a different province. It's amazing what you can tell by just looking at someone, and the effect if you show a little kinship, and tenderness.' I smiled at my father; my father smiled at me.

I am driving quite slowly now. The car has moved well onto the road's shoulder. I nod, my audience unseen, as if to say, You see – he's funny. And then the old nostalgia, that seductive immediacy, the rushing aliveness, the sadness washes over me, and I sigh. Like a man emerging from a high.

PALIMPSEST

Years ago my mother returns from a visit to the farm, to see her sister. She seems fine. But something is off. She is listless, for weeks, but not quite depressed. She tells me, later – much later – that she was trying to find a way to suggest that we kill ourselves.

Years ago my father is asleep on a couch. It is late in the night and I switch off the lamp next to his head. He wakes up, a look of terror on his face. He is not awake yet; he is terrified, quietly terrified, pulls back his hand in a fist. A moment later he is fully awake, he relaxes. He lowers his hand, away from me. He apologises, says he had been dreaming.

I am the son of fragile parents. They live emotional lives, they feel deeply, with great immediacy. And so I must not be fragile. The child learns to invert the dynamic: feel deeply, but correct for emotion, keep it in check. Extremity of feeling is to be resisted; it begets anxiety, then rage (him), or depression (her).

The child becomes the adult – early – to both. For her: protect her from bad news, sources of anxiety; keep her even, contented. For him: protect yourself from the dark incipience; do not acknowledge extremity, keep things light, maintain distance; there must be no licence to get close. Disconnect. Realign the wiring.

Yes, I think my parents would have preferred a more passionate son. Someone more connected to emotion, more fearlessly spontaneous. But look where all your feeling, your passion, your spontaneity got you.

And so with them I am calm, coolly distant. I am acquiescent, polite, pliant, mature. Careful. Care. Full.

My father and I drive through the rain to buy fish and chips, on a Friday evening when I am a boy. He tells me stories. He tells the story of a group of people – maybe a family, but possibly not – who invite a guest to dinner. Slowly it is revealed that the guest had done something horrible to all of them, years before. But they keep it light, they say all is forgiven. They keep at it, they share the detail, in increments, over wine. There are anecdotes with sharp, hard edges. They laugh too loudly. At the end of the meal the guest excuses himself and hangs himself in the bathroom. They have dessert, in silence, then phone the police.

Years later I think of enacting the story. I want to remember everything. I want to weaponise words. I want to tell the truth. I want to do it dispassionately. I want to print the words, and send them to him. All neatly bound in a volume. I'll include a rope.

An author tells me there is only one story to each of us. What is our essential narrative? I think mine is the need to connect, but also the fear of doing so.

Another author tells me there has been an end to history, to the progress of ideas. At an individual level, does one's history stop when one discovers the individual narrative of self? No further evolution. Remembering. Re-membering. Simply repetition. Repeat. Repeat.

GREY

There is a religious fundamentalist on the periphery of my life, in my circle of acquaintances. She is resolute: solid and serene as a mid-ocean wave. She never compromises. Her judgements are sure and immutable. She offends and injures with impunity. She has cosmic licence to do this, because she knows The Truth. And didn't Christ also stand alone? She lives in the white; sinners live in the black. There is no grey.

I dislike her intensely. My response to her is excessive civility. We smile at each other and pointedly (as if by mutual agreement) never discuss anything real. I am quite certain that she loathes me too. She condemns and pities me, in an indistinct, satisfied way, because from her perspective I languish in the black; I am doomed to rot and roil for all time.

But she is wrong. I too would prefer the bold conviction, the splendid aesthetic and moral clarity, of white. It is the safety of moral certainty that is most seductive – more so, even, than achieving purity of colour. But life is lived in the space between white and black: grey so often dominates.

* * *

In my parents' first year of marriage my father becomes smitten and cultivates a relationship with a young intellectual. She will soon surpass him with her abundant talent and critical acclaim. It is not clear to me whether their emotional affair is ever consummated. I do know how my mother feels about the woman, about having to serve them tea and then excuse herself, get out of their way, and so, as I grow up I steer clear; I never ask my mother for more information. She and my father were constructed clearly in my mind, in shiny lacquer black.

When I am twenty-five years old I attend a conference. She is in attendance. I walk up to her, nod hello. I see her recognise another twenty-five-year-old with my face, from a lifetime ago. She looks down at my name tag, and the knowledge is confirmed. Although neither of us acknowledge the past, or common denominators, we are interested in each other, and so for three days we sit next to each other, we roll our eyes at the presentations, we make little jokes, we share peppermints.

At the end of the conference we say goodbye. We have no reason to remain in touch – and we do not. One bogey from my youth has become something else. She is transformed, somehow, from black space into something not quite white.

* * *

For my sixth birthday my mother arranges for a small group of children from Clarens to have a party at Loch Lomond lake, thirty kilometres away, just outside Bethlehem. There are not many children (certainly no more than ten), and being the children of my parents' social group, they are of varying ages, from my own age up to ten and eleven years.

There is a pair of fraternal twins, a boy and a girl, of around nine years old. I do not remember their names. What I do remember is running next to the lake, looking up at the boy, and experiencing a feeling that I am unable to name, but which I know – even at that age – I should not discuss with anyone. The feeling lives in the black; it is not permitted.

I only remember meeting up with the twins one more time, on a school trip to a farm, maybe one year later. We are tasked to pick bunches of cosmos. The boy and I are by ourselves, on the edge of a wheatfield. There is some great unspoken, something unnameable, between us. At the end of our thirty minutes of flower picking, I give him half of my bunch. The boy looks at my gift, takes the flowers from me and leans down, gives me a quick, chaste kiss on the lips. We join the others at the waiting bus. That is all.

It was something innocent and beautiful – but also, somehow, not.

* * *

When I am eleven years old my parents divorce each other for a second and final time. By now my father has been mostly absent from the family home for some years, so there is no dramatic before-and-after. If anything, there is a more formalised sense of relief.

But the day of the divorce itself is hard. I watch my mother arrive home, early that evening. She drives up in her small silver car and parks outside the garage door, switches off the engine. She remains seated with the car door closed, breathing and blinking in the silence. I can see that she is in a dark space, although she has set up the day as a liberation, with a promise of unlimited fish fingers, chips, and mayonnaise, for dinner. The day is supposed to be washed in white, but it is very dark.

I have a plan to make her feel better. I turn away from the window and thumb through the vinyl record collection, selecting Mendelssohn's Violin Concerto in E minor, Opus 64. Keeping an eye on the door, I put the needle right at the end. Timing is everything. There is a small cadenza near the end of the movement when the woodwinds play the main tune against prolonged trills from the solo violin. The concerto concludes with a frenetic coda, which includes what my mother still refers to as one of the most beautiful notes in all of music. And that is what she hears when she opens the door. My timing is perfect.

My mother is quietly emotional (no tears), hugging me close. She asks me to put the concerto on from the start, and moves to the kitchen to prepare our meal. We do not talk much. The day is not quite white, but not quite dark either.

* * *

Moving to a small rural town far away from the city is transformative. Aged nine, I am able to leave much darkness behind, and explore the light. Some of this consists of adjusting one's persona. It is like acting a new part in a play: the city boy from far away; the purveyor of an exotic accent, a foreign vocabulary, a different kind of past.

This new stage holds much promise. I have a romantic idea of rural life, of small-town, provincial people somehow more essentially good, light. For the most part I am correct. Our neighbour is Tannie Suzie, who is ancient and whose backdoor stoep is visible from our own. She spends her afternoons listening to radio dramas, knitting, drinking tea, and eating rusks.

She invites me over and feeds me homemade treats. I lie on my back in the Little Karoo sun and listen to Tannie Suzie's anecdotes about life in the 1930s, when she was a girl. I adore her. She is the grandmother I never had, the one I can trust. She is uncomplicated, innocent, and wise. She exemplifies unconditional love.

One afternoon in the early winter she notes the change in temperature, and tells me about a poor coloured fellow she once discovered sleeping in her garden shed. She chased him away, declined his request for something to eat, and the next day she heard that he was found frozen to death by the river. She feels bad about that. She offers me more biscuits, which I accept.

Until then adults are easy to classify: mother – good, white light; Evelina – good, white light; all others – not to be trusted, no light.

But Tannie Suzie poses a particular challenge. I love her so very much, but there is this darkness about her too. Can I live with it, and love her still? Yes, I find that I can.

* * *

At the end of therapy, right before I leave for Paris, the therapist Sarah takes me to breakfast. We are celebrating nearly three years of hard work – we have achieved much. At the end, Sarah gives me a warning: she says that, sometimes but not always, people with my kind of background find sustained regular interaction boring, and that in life I may find myself seeking out dysfunction. Sarah quotes Dorothy Parker: 'They sicken of the calm who know the storm.' I nod that I understand, and tell Sarah that I'll watch out.

Recently I discover a new recording of Robert Palmer's old song 'Johnny and Mary'. This version is slower, and is delivered in Bryan Ferry's mysterious, liquid voice, telling us of Johnny who needs all the world to confirm that he's not lonely, trying to find certainty.

I put this on repeat, in the car, driving home after work. It is not dysfunction I want, not at all. That is a promise to Sarah I can keep. If anything, my inclination has been in the other direction: trying to find certainty. I want the white, but at the same time I distrust it. It is the grey that dominates, in life. And maybe that is how it should be.

I think again about my religious fundamentalist acquaintance. I do not loathe her. I do despise her moralism, and her cruelty. But on another level, part of the truth is that I envy her. I wish I had her certainty.

11:03

On Thursday 3 November 1983 at 11:03 a.m. exactly I am standing under a tree, alone during breaktime, the new boy in a new school, and I make a promise to myself. I turned eleven a few weeks ago, and my life is a shambles. We have recently moved back to a city I hate, possibly to a parent who scares me very much, and I have become so accustomed to turmoil and the vicissitudes of kinship that I have developed a physical essential tremor. And in all of this, after I eat my solitary sandwich, wishing that breaktime would be over, I press my thumb and hold it gently on a spot on a tree branch, at the exact place where a smaller branch or a twig has been amputated, long ago, as a way to mark and soothe that spot. A moment later I look at my watch, which is a new digital one (maybe I got it for my birthday), and I then switch the setting from the time, which reads '11:03', to the date, which, coincidentally, also reads '11:03'. Prone to magical thinking, I take this as a sign that I am experiencing a Moment Of Significance. I promise myself that, from that day on, every year on 3 November, I will look at my watch at 11:03, and celebrate the person I am right then, and recall my touch of the tree's scar. And so for nearly four decades that is what I have been doing. And I know this is silly and whimsical – I do not even wear a watch any more – but I have kept it up. These days I set my phone to go off at exactly that time, every year on 3 November. And from way back in 1983 I smile towards my current self, and I so, so wish that I, now, can touch that boy gently with my thumb, the way I did that tree. But maybe, in my way, I do.

ACCRETION

I cannot see him and so I approach the host, or manager, who is biting the tip of a pencil and looking at rows of numbers near the cash register.

'I'm looking for my brother,' I say. 'I know he's arrived because he's sent me a WhatsApp, but I can't see him at the tables on the floor – do you have a separate seating area?'

She looks me up and down, then past me, behind me, into the distance. 'Looks like you, but a younger model?' she asks.

Her description pleases me, and I nod, smiling. She motions with her chin, behind me, and when I turn around I see him jogging across the lawn towards me. Yes – looks like me, but a younger model: my brother.

This is last Sunday afternoon, and we are meeting to celebrate the one-year anniversary of our reacquaintance.

'Wanted to check out the tree over there,' he explains. 'Sorry I am late.'

'You're not late,' I say, and Ben lifts his arms and hugs me, as we have come to do when we say hello, and when we say goodbye. Once we sit down I can look at him properly. His eyes are clear and he is relaxed, friendly; we are happy to be with each other; we have come far in one year. Ben manages the condiments and passes me what I need; by now he does not need to ask me what I want. We are a small, unspoken bureaucracy of kinship and familiarity.

Once our sandwiches and our coffees are to our liking, we touch the paper cups – a casual toast – and take a sip. He tells me about his Buddhist retreat; I tell him about work, and things at home. Ben and I are planning a road trip somewhere, and after that a train journey somewhere else; we have brought our diaries with us to see what is possible. We decide on a trip to Sutherland, soonish, for stargazing, which interests both of us.

We both seek out spontaneous engagement with things, with life – experiences unfiltered by intrusive thoughts or personal editorialising – and we have, some time ago, decided that this is more easily achievable when we pursue activities that are aesthetically or sensually pleasing. Ben tells me that he looks for quiet openness, without the intrusion of interpretation, in meditation.

'As long as we don't look for it at the bottom of a bottle,' I say, rather unthinkingly, but Ben does not flinch.

'Meaning,' he says, 'is accretion.' I want to say something but I can tell my brother is not done, and so I take a sip of my drink instead. He changes his mind, takes a bite of his sandwich and chews.

I say to Ben that I make most meaning in my life through these meetings of ours, that I am so very grateful to have him in my life. My psychologist friend has told me not to expect similar expressions of affection from Ben, but I should also know that, although he may seem incapable of expressing it, he really craves and appreciates it. I remain quiet for a second, and then I tell him that this joy, this wonderful development in my life, also has a cost – the fear that I will lose him again.

'I have a great need to drink in every second, to process it, to savour it, because I love these meetings, and I love you, brother,' I tell him, 'but it comes with a need to record it, to filter it, because it may be impermanent. Every time may be the last time.'

'I am not going anywhere,' Ben announces matter-of-factly. 'I am your brother forever, even when I am not with you.'

What he says distracts me, makes me think of something else, as I recall something my mother told me, years and years ago, about unfound treasures never truly being lost. Ben looks at me, and for a moment I see the eight-year-old boy pushing a slab of chocolate into my back trouser pocket, as I wave at the others from the airport boarding gate before my departure to Paris, well over twenty years ago.

Then he looks at my plate and says, 'Can we swop olives?' The salad that came with his sandwich contains only green olives, of which he is not fond. I nod, and so he transfers the green ones to my plate, and takes my black olives. I do not say anything. Instead, I take a bite of my food; my preference is also for black olives, but this is what older brothers do, apparently – or rather, this is what we do for people we love.

I consider what he said, about meaning. 'For a long time,' I tell Ben, 'I was petrified of any relationship with you, or with others. I found safety in the absence of contact – not from you, of course, but from the rest of it, from everything it invited in. Now that there is contact again, I have to remember and reinterpret so much. I have to remeaning it, continuously. Yes, meaning is accretion, but I have to unlayer and review and relayer so many things. I've lost so many of my certainties.'

For the first time Ben and I really talk about our father. This is something we have avoided. We have used the past year to get to know each other, as cleanly as possible, as individuals, without starting with or basing it on what or whom we have in common genetically. But today we talk about Dad. This starts with me telling Ben that I've read up about half-siblings; I have discovered that, genetically, he and I are as related to each other as we are to our father.

'I guess that makes sense,' Ben announces, after a moment's reflection.

'Yes I suppose so,' I say.

I take out my phone and I show Ben a photograph of our dad when he was in the army. Dad is lying on a bed, reading. There is a pipe in his mouth and he is wearing black-rimmed glasses. My brother looks at the image for a long time.

'Please send it to me,' he asks. I forward the photo to him straight away, and he inspects it on his own phone. Again, I am struck by the fact that Ben never knew his father as a young man. I tell him it's a pity he didn't know Dad when he was young. Sure, the dark things were much more pointed, and the edges sharper, but he also carried in him such energy and joy – he ate life.

'I was so lucky to have Dad,' Ben tells me, 'especially during the worst times of my depression. He took such good care of me. I am so glad now to have a chance to take care of him.' Ben goes on: 'I think you saw the worst of him. I do not know the detail, but I know things were very rough while you were growing up.'

I have to proceed carefully. I am at a crossroads. I tell my brother that I could tell him some of those things, but I would prefer not to. What good can possibly come of it? He's already caring for this unwell, isolated, alienated old man – all by himself, no one to help. I tell my brother that I'd so like to help him – Ben – in some way, to reduce the burden somehow, but I just cannot allow this man into my life again.

'I want to care for and be good for you,' I tell Ben, 'but I can't do that for Dad.' He observes me passively, undemanding, and tells me that he gets it completely, that he's fine, that he doesn't need any help.

'Maybe I can give you a sense of him as a young man,' I say. 'There were incredible moments of tenderness, of grace, and of poignancy, and they were made all the more meaningful because of the contrast with his more destructive behaviour. Dad showed me hell, and took me there, but he also showed me heaven. Dad gave me the two extremes of the spectrum – it's the middle I never had, and which I craved.'

'I had the middle,' says Ben. 'But not many of the dark extremes that you saw.' And not much joy at all, I think to myself, because of the addictions: Dad has been drifting in a grey soup of increasing distance and sadness these past twenty-five years, increasingly and more or less permanently tranquillised.

We finish our meal. Ben is parked at the very far end of the parking area, and so I drive him there. While we drive, we chat about our Sutherland plans. When we get to his bakkie we get out and continue our conversation, both of us leaning against our respective vehicles. At the end of it, we hug. At the exit he turns left, to go and prepare dinner for a frail old man; I turn right, in the opposite direction.

We are siblings temporally misaligned. We know the same man, the same father, but both of us have missing data, different and differently lived experiences. We will help each other with our respective deficits. I can tell him about the young man, about the terrifying and magnificent acuity, about extremity of experience; I shall focus on the joy, and poignancy – what good is there in exposing the violence and the wounds, gnawing at that hangnail and making it kitsch? For what? To teach him to hate the man he loves? Why would I do that?

And maybe he will teach me about the older father. About how he mellowed into maturity. About little extremity of feeling, but about more moments of peace (I hope). And yes, there is now a kind of absence of joy – but also less rage.

We are, Ben and I, each other's memories; we are the missing strips of narrative recording that have fallen to the cutting room floors of our lives.

We will try to close the circle more fully, and make meaning for each other along the way.

We do this with care, gently, and with tenderness – we are brotherly amanuenses: layering, filtering, adding, adding, adding.

UNQUIET

Let me tell you about silence.

Recently I sat in a Cape Town brasserie waiting for Ben. It was his birthday – his thirtieth – and so we had arranged to do something special together. In our book, that means having a burger and a milkshake at a hipster place on Loop Street. I was early, so I ordered a drink while I waited for Ben to arrive from his conference.

My conversation with the waiter (bored, resentful, no eye contact) went more or less as follows:

'What smoothies do you have?'

'Mango. And strawberry.'

'Mango-*and*-strawberry – or mango, *or* strawberry?'

'Mango, or strawberry.'

'I'll have the mango smoothie, please.'

'We're out of mango pulp.'

'I'll have a glass of sparkling water, please.'

I was still smiling about this when two young women arrived, selecting seats two tables down from where I was. It was late afternoon; we were the only clients.

'I know, right?'

'And she's back with him?'

'She always goes back to him.'

'He's such a shit. Everyone knows he beats her. Everyone can see how he treats her.'

'And she gobbles it up.'

'I guess it's *luuuurve*.'

'Well, it's something.'

'Can't help her if she doesn't say something. Just wallows in that silence. Her brave little shrugs.'

I picked up my glass and gestured to the waiter that I was moving to the first floor. He shrugged.

So, let me tell you something about silence. And about brave little shrugs.

It is somewhere towards the middle of 1983. I am ten years old. My father is visiting us in Oudtshoorn, but this week we are in Mossel Bay. We are renting a beach shack near the Point, just behind the rock pools and the large tidal pool on the other side of the swings. There is a whole row of these ramshackle little wooden houses. Most of them are empty now, because it is off season, so we have the small shale beach and the rocks almost to ourselves.

We know no one, and we now live in a part of the country where we find it hard to follow the language, because it sounds so different. We are alone in the world. And now he is here with us.

On this particular morning my mother and I are standing in a rock pool, our feet in the water, looking down. My father – drunk, or high, or both – is in the shack, about twenty metres away. We are allowed to go as far as the rock pools without him; any further and he will shoot the dog, Bruni, who is in the shack with him. To a distant observer it may look as though my mother and I are collecting sea-shells. In truth, she is trying to catch her own reflection in the water, to see how bad it is. She has been lucky; only two blows really found their target.

Because we are not allowed to go out, to go grocery shopping, we have to make do with the food that we have. We had planned to be at the shack for only a longish weekend, but by now (well into the next week) food options are limited. My mother used what was available: breakfast was scrambled eggs with leftover pasta. It wasn't bad. But it gave my father the pretext he needed, to belittle her, to escalate, and so he smashed the plate against the wall, and as she bent down to pick up the shards before the dog could get to them, he kicked her in the stomach – hard. She was winded, gasping for breath, and as she steadied herself on her arm, to get up from the floor, his fist found her eye socket.

I jumped to get between them, but my mother, still wheezing, still trying to get up, shook her head at me, moving to get his attention away from me.

'Nee, Pappa!' I shouted, forcing my way between them. I was a tall boy, but no match for him. Also, I was paralysed by fear. There was the fear of the physical pain he was inflicting, the chaos, but mostly I was afraid he was going to strangle or shoot her – and that I may survive.

He looked at me, bored, indifferent. He went down on his haunches, so our eyes were close.

'Nee, Pappa; nee, Pappa; nee, Pappa,' he whispered to me, smiling.

But this was long enough for the change to happen, for the retreat to be activated. It worked like this: my father's violence was cyclical. He would either drink steadily, relentlessly, or he would take the pills and the alcohol together, in one large gulp. Usually he was very good at pacing himself. There was an unspoken tipping point, and then he required a trigger, to escalate. Usually he achieved this by trapping my mother in an endless conversation, asking her questions, increasing the pressure and criticism of who she was, what she believed, her family, her background, until she was unable to answer him – and then he would strike.

But then, once the physical violence was lanced, he would retreat. Not for long, though. He would stagger away from the violence he had perpetrated, as though he himself was shocked by it, or rather, in awe of it, and he would shrink to bed, or the couch, with a bottle. And there he would suckle for an hour or two, but not before he forced my mother to join him on the bed, or on the couch, and he would make sure that she did not go anywhere. And as long as he had her, he had me. Often, in these circumstances, he would lock me out of the room they were in, or out of the house altogether, for hours. Marital rape did not exist then, even in whispers. I would sit and wait. And listen. Petrified. All I could do was pray and pray and pray, into the silence.

This morning we were lucky to get out of the shack. This time he decided to sit in a rocking chair, the dog by his feet, the revolver on the small table next to the bottle, and allow the two of us to walk down to the water together. He was watching us from where he sat.

'I can't see any blood,' I say cheerily, happy to deliver the good news. 'But it's all swollen. And the colour is weird.'

My mother is holding her stomach with her one arm, breathing carefully, feeling herself, her ribs, to see if she is still all there.

'I'm fine, darling, really, it's not so bad,' she says, smiling at me, dark glasses in place. 'We'll tell people that I slipped in the rock pool, and that I caught my eye on your elbow. Okay?'

'Yes,' I nod. That seems to me like a splendid idea. My smile is real: I am delighted, because if she thinks there will be people, later on, to placate with a lie, to keep away with silence, then that means she thinks we may survive this. There is a chance he is not going to kill us. The planning of a lie, for later on, means there is reason to hope.

And survive we did. But first we needed to escape. By now it was clear to my mother that the violence was escalating badly. With that gun in the mix all variables became uncertain, loose little vectors of malice. It came down to a simple calculation: there was more than sufficient alcohol and pills in the house for him to feed the monster, and the violence. We did not have enough food to keep going, for him to feed on and to metabolise the drugs. There were not enough people around, not enough people of the right kind, to appeal to. (Families and couples were useless, because they tended to be shocked, and look away. Men were the worst: they would shake their heads, as if in anger, and do nothing.) And whom would we ask? We knew no one. There was no one to phone, even if we could get to a payphone.

I do not remember the beach shack having any windows. This is absurd, because all houses have windows. I know this in the abstract, in principle. But this house in my mind was in shadow. Maybe there were windows, but the curtains remained drawn shut. I remember the darkness, and how carefully we stepped on the floorboards: if we woke him up, a new cycle of terror would begin. Silence was best; silence meant that we were surviving. With my mother trapped indoors with him, he sometimes gave me coins to use to cross the road and to drive the go-carts in the fun park. From there – no other kids around, the caretaker an old toothless man – I would drive around and around, watching the shack. It is creepy, to be outside a dwelling, even a friendly one, a holiday home, and just watch it. It is so quiet. It is so entirely silent, impervious to regard. Nothing moves. Who knows what is going on inside? But I know. And I cannot go looking for help, because if he does not hear the metallic whining of that go-cart, he will strangle her in the silence. So, I drive the circuit. Around, and around, and around.

'We're over there,' I say to the old man, handing over my coins, motioning towards the shack with my head. 'My mom and my dad and the dog and I. We're in there.'

I look at the man and smile one of my polite little smiles, and he says 'Uh-huh, ja, I know.' And I give a little shrug, and wave as I walk away, into what he is unable to see.

There are other worlds folded right into the one we live in. We are surrounded by them. We cannot see them, but they are right here. Unless someone tells, unless they say something, one does not really know what is going on in the car driving right past you when you are in traffic. People look at you from behind screens or through the windows of houses and you are unable to know what is really happening. I look at my primary school class photographs of that time. That is me in the back row, in the middle; straight hair and polite smile; a little pale, because I do not go outside much. And I'm in hell.

My mother's plan is risky. For it to work, he needs to get friendly-drunk; she needs to control the pace. Drugs and alcohol make you strong, up to a point. And then it takes you and you pass out. My mother needs to calibrate him precisely. She splashes out on the remaining food: the contents of sausages are pushed into a pan, and she fries it with what is left over of the onions and the garlic. She pours the last of the smoked tomato paste into the pan and toasts the last of the bread; she uses the bacon pan grease as butter. She is hoping that the strength of these aromas will be sufficient to cover the taste of the tranquilliser she has crushed into his portion. It is a strange, last supper. If he eats well, if he likes the food, that is one fewer trigger he can use. She keeps his glass full, from one of those infinite green Culemborg bottles. She keeps him on wine, which means that he is getting drunk more slowly, but the dip will be more profound, once the drug kicks in; also, it postpones the violence that will follow when he switches to harder stuff. The timing has to be just right.

My job is a background one, but very important. As I am invisible to my father, only ever used as a prop to control or torture my mother, I have greater freedom of movement. We've planned it all down at the rock pool: little signals she will give me, actions I need to perform that can save us or doom us. I have to get the car keys from where he keeps them on top of the cupboard in their bedroom. She is talking warmly with him, in the kitchen, and I move the chair in the bedroom over to the cupboard, I get onto it and for a moment it wobbles beneath me. I feel around for the keys with my one hand while I keep the door in my line of sight. Through the crack I can see my father cradling the revolver like a Fabergé egg, talking to my mother, smiling at her compliments.

I have the keys. I put them in my trouser pocket, making sure they don't make a sound. I return the chair where it belongs. I breathe deeply, to seem calm, and I walk into the room where they are. I have to get to the car outside and unlock the driver and the front passenger doors, check that the rear car doors remain locked, and insert the key in the ignition so that it's ready for our getaway. The car is in the driveway, right outside the back door, a few steps across the stoep; it is facing away from the main road, in front of the shack, but there is a small road that runs right around the shack; if we can manage to start the car and get going, that small road will take us around the little house and onto the way towards escape. I don't bother with the house keys and my mother's handbag or purse; if we do manage to escape, we will think of a way to get into the house, in Oudtshoorn. The important thing now is to get away.

I enter the room and I nod a confirmation to my mother, who understands that I have the keys. I have about half a minute to get the dog out of the house with me and into the car, then I will lock my car door on the inside, open the driver's door wide, and wait for her.

My father glances up at me, mid-sentence, but looks away. I yawn, I look down, I stroll slowly towards the back door.

'Kom Bruni, kom piepie,' I tell the dog. My father accepts this, makes no move to stop me. He's in the middle of some kind of rhetorical point to my mother.

The dog gets up from near my father and strolls towards me, tail wagging. I open the door and let her out; she waits for me right outside the door. Good dog.

With my left hand I manage to switch the automatic lock on the door into the 'lock' position. This means that, when my mother slams shut that door behind her, on her way out, the lock will catch, and if my father then tries to open it, he'll have to pause, to unlock it with both hands. At the very least, he'll have to move the gun to his other hand, or into a pocket, to do so. That'll win us one or two seconds, for my mother to run around the car and get into the driver's seat.

Everything slows down.

'Kom, Bruni,' I say, opening the car door as softly as I can. The dog listens, she jumps into the car. I slowly, soundlessly pull my passenger door shut, and lock it. I make sure the rear car doors are locked. I push the ignition key into the starter. I unlock the driver's door and open it wide, from the inside. I hold my right arm across the space between the two front seats, to keep the dog in the back. I turn and look at the shack's door.

She must have done something to distract him from what was happening right behind him, right outside the back door. His back is turned to me, and I can now see that what she'd done was to open the cold-water tap; the water is rushing noisily into the metal basin. He can't hear. She has line of sight of what I'm doing in the car. I nod at her. We're ready.

She keeps the water running and casually walks around the table, all the while talking to him, and moves towards the cupboard with the plates. She makes a movement as though she is gathering something, to lay the table in front of him, but instead of turning back to him (the water still going) she keeps walking, without haste, in my direction.

Everything slows down.

She reaches the door before he turns around. She steps outside and slams the door, hard, behind her.

And then she runs.

She is in the car next to me.

My father is to my left, trying to open the passenger door. The car shakes from side to side as he pulls violently on my door, then the back door. He is running around the car, behind the back, to get to the other doors.

There is a lot of noise. It is me, screaming at my mother to Go, Go, Go, Go.

He manages to open the hatchback, but before he can jump into the car we're moving, the tyres spinning, mud everywhere, and we're going forwards, then around the house, and I can't see him any more.

By the time we round the house and get to the front, to turn onto the road that will take us out of the crescent street, he is coming around the house from the other side. My mother accelerates. We pass him. We scream. We laugh. We've done it.

We laugh and scream and laugh and scream. I only notice that I'd pissed my pants when we reach the main road.

I do not remember the rest of the trip, or the logistics of our arrival in Oudtshoorn, an hour and a half later. But I do remember my mother's terror, and then mine: we're petrified he'll alert the authorities; there'll be a roadblock and the police will wait for us at the main intersection outside Mossel Bay, and return us to him. But of course there is no roadblock. There are no police. We are free.

By the time we get home, the rules are in place. This entire episode is 'Huisdinge': our code word for things that can never be discussed with anyone. We cannot trust anyone else, because they live in a different world. They live in a world of weekend braais, or sport on the television on Saturday afternoons. It is a world that I imagine is like living inside *The Waltons*, where John-Boy and his father always somehow keep poverty at bay, and where no adversity upsets them, because they have love, and trust, and warmth. That is a world of fiction.

Instead, we live in the world of Huisdinge. We remain silent. The world out there is the world of chaos, and of not understanding. How do we even begin to describe or express what we know? There simply is no vocabulary. 'Domestic violence' comes nowhere close; it is meaningless before the reality of the terror. Even if we are able to find words to express our reality, the fucking humiliation will destroy us. We are so isolated, so alienated, so alone, that we have forgotten or unlearnt regular patterns of interaction. 'Normal' does not exist. There is no trust possible. Silence will keep us safe. Silence is intimate. Silence is solidarity. And the unspoken horror is so much more immediate than the unsafe narratives outside of us.

Huisdinge becomes so pervasive that I nearly stop talking altogether, by my early teens. I'm not weird or anything – I am perfectly capable of delivering an oral in a language class, or of speaking full sentences when spoken to. But I never volunteer. I am always polite. I am meticulously attuned to the emotions and small signals of those around me, and I calibrate my own every single second. My main goal is never to upset, to live in the invisible, in the quiet. It becomes addictive, and so safe. Yes, it feels a little dead, everyone becomes distant, but if nothing happens, then you are safe. And safety is the most precious thing.

By the time I am thirteen years old, I am so quiet that my mother forces me to take the job as tour guide at one of the local ostrich farms, to get me to talk to other people. For extra money, all I really want to do is to wash the dishes at the local Spur, or to water the plants at the nursery around the corner, or to comb the Angora rabbits on the rabbit farm on the way to the Cango Caves. These jobs will give me what I want: no one to talk to, no real conversation required, safe inside myself; I want a life where I can drift in celestial silence, invisible and quiet as a rogue planet, divorced from any home star. But my mother knows these traps, and so she forces me to talk, to get a job where I have to talk. I hate it. I detest her for making me do this. But after only a few months my teachers remark to her that I have now started to speak above a whisper, in class. It is working. She has broken my silence.

And I know all of this is a kind of pornography. Look at this wound. Let me show you that bruise. It is embarrassing. It is inappropriate. It is over-disclosive.

But here's the thing: I now know the power of naming, of saying, of speaking it. I know the abundant evil of not pointing at evil and saying 'evil'. I will not be silenced again. I refuse to be complicit in my own terror, by not speaking its name. I will speak it, I will describe it, I will shout it, I will scream it. I encourage others to do this, but I know it is not easy for them; I will try not to be too hard on their silences, and their little shrugs.

* * *

After our burgers and milkshakes, on his birthday, Ben and I drive to Rondebosch. He needs to make up his mind whether he will meet his friends and allow them to treat him to birthday drinks, or whether instead he will go to the Buddhist centre just down the road from the restaurant, to meditate for a few hours.

Ben tells me that he needs this meditation. He craves it like oxygen. He loves the silence. He loves that way of drawing into himself, and the safety, and the freedom of disconnect. He wants the quiet.

His phone rings, as we pass UCT. It is his friends. They want to know if he is coming. Ben tells them he will let them know in five minutes.

My brother looks out the window on his side of the car and I can see him thinking.

'They love you,' I say to him. 'They want to be with you.'

My brother looks at me.

'You should let them love you. Go be with them,' I say. 'You can go to meditation tomorrow.'

My brother reflects for a second, then WhatsApps his friend: 'See you in three.' Then he nods at me, smiles.

I park the car, but I keep the engine running. I get out to hug my brother before he walks into the restaurant. He thanks me for the time together, for the chat, and the gift.

As he turns to go, I say to him, 'You know, to be silent and to be quiet are not the same things.'

'I know,' he says.

BREAD AND FLOWERS

Recently, I am in Cape Town, to meet up with a visiting academic, but I am using the opportunity to see Ben. We have not seen each other in a few months, so I am not sure what to expect. As soon as I see him, though, I relax: his eyes are clear, bright blue, and his body is relaxed when I hug him.

He tells me that Dad has been ill; in June or July, Ben thought it was the end, and it was hard to manage, because Dad refuses to co-operate. I tell Ben I am sorry that I cannot do more to help him with all of that. Ben shrugs, says it is no problem. I struggle to find out what exactly was the issue, why it was so serious, but Ben tells me it was something to do with his balance. I do not quite follow, and then Ben says he has been spending regular periods of time at his mother's beach house, to escape. I am still curious about Ben's dad's health, but I let that go.

Ben uses the word 'escape' a few times, when he describes his own retreat from his father; he is considering going to Japan, to get away from everything. I nod encouragingly, sipping my latte, and Ben adds that it is quite possible that Japan will happen next year or the year after. This is a pragmatic, hopeful declaration, but the implication of what needs to happen hangs unsubtly in the air between us.

'And how are you?' Ben asks me, after he has told me about himself.

I lift my face towards him, in surprise, and then he adds, 'And how is your mom?' I smile at this, at the novelty of it, and I wonder where this interest comes from. I tell him about work, about people at work and at home, and we talk about arthritis in elderly parents. When I remark on how well he is looking, Ben says that he exercises more, and that he is redesigning the whole of his mother's back garden.

'It's your mom's birthday today,' I say.

'Seriously?' Ben asks. I nod. I ask him if he'll see her later today.

'Yes,' he says, distracted. 'What can I get her?' he asks me. I suggest that he picks up some fresh flowers at the flower market in Adderley Street.

'Will that be enough?' he asks, worried. I tell him the flowers will be fine. Ben nods. 'I'm so glad you told me it's her birthday,' he says.

When we get back to his life in general, he tells me that he has been going to a therapist, for one hour every two weeks, and that this seems to be going well.

'How did you find your way to a therapist?' I ask, aware of Ben's difficulty in finding someone who resonates with him.

'Oh, I'm playing the guitar again, a bit, with an old high school teacher of mine, and he got me in touch with the therapist.'

'This is all very good, Ben,' I say, meaning it. My brother nods at the truth of this. I am careful not to over-express my delight about the therapist, so I let that go. We talk about the music, the guitar he wants to buy, and about the creative process.

The waiter asks us what we want to eat. We are at a novelty bakery, specialising in bread. I dislike menus, and since it is mid-morning I order the poached eggs with a croissant, and a loaf of sourdough bread on the side, which I will take away with me. Ben studies the menu carefully. The waiter goes off to clear another table; he will be back for our order in a minute.

'What is a roulade?' Ben asks, and I tell him it is a piece of rolled meat, or pastry, and that it can be savoury or sweet, depending on the dish. This seems to satisfy Ben, who orders a single piece of salmon roulade, and a single piece of chicken roulade.

'Is that it?' the waiter asks.

'Yes, thank you,' Ben says. We order fresh coffees.

'So listen, I have two things to tell you,' I say to him.

Ben looks at me and I count my agenda down on two fingers.

'The first thing is an apology. The second thing is to ask your permission, or rather, to get your opinion about something.'

Ben looks interested.

While we talk the food arrives. My brother inspects the two modest rolled pieces of meat on his plate. He asks me if he can cut off and eat some of the sourdough loaf that the waiter has placed next to my plate of food. I nod, and as I talk Ben stands up and cuts a chunk from the end of the loaf. I tell him it is an interesting combination of peasant bread and hoity-toity meat, which seems to amuse him. He nods again, chewing, and gives me his attention.

'So, my apology first,' I say. 'The way I remembered our lack of contact has been all wrong, Ben. For all these years, or rather, over the course of all these years I gradually came to believe my own fiction, that we simply fell out of touch, with me in Joburg and you in Cape Town, and then when I moved overseas contact became even more unlikely.'

Ben nods at me, unconcerned.

'But it's not entirely true,' I continue. 'When you were around sixteen or seventeen years old your mom phoned me and asked me to be more in touch with you, as a positive male role model, and I tried that for a bit, but it didn't quite work, you and me, and I then really abandoned you. I didn't keep at it, I didn't keep on pursuing contact.'

My brother looks at me, chewing impassively, and so I say, 'I am sorry,' and stop talking.

Ben shrugs, sniffs, and blows his nose on a paper serviette.

'Well,' he says, sipping more coffee, 'that was when my depression was really taking off. I was completely out of it. No contact was possible.' When I look at Ben, saying nothing, he says, 'So relax.' He shrugs again. 'The contact we have now would not have been possible until about two or three years ago.' I can see he means this, that he is not simply placating me or being kind. I nod and smile at him.

'Will flowers be enough?' he asks, suddenly worried. 'For my mom.' I tell him flowers will be fine. Ben nods. 'I am so glad you told me it is her birthday,' he says again.

'What is the thing you wanted to ask me?' he says.

I lower my voice and look down at my hands.

'I have been writing about you, and about things that have happened to you, and to me, and about Dad. I don't want to hurt you by writing the things that I write about Dad, but I feel justified to do so, because it is my story.' I look at Ben, who is watching me evenly. 'But it is also your story – parts of it, anyway – and you love Dad, and therefore you should know that I'm doing this. I try to be as candid as possible, and I sometimes make reference to very personal things, like your diagnosis, or mine. I am torn about asking your permission, because if you were to say no to me, I will probably continue to do it anyway, but I want you to be aware of it, especially as this story may be published.'

I stop talking, and spread my hands out on the table in front of me, as a way to demonstrate that I have finished.

'I wish I was more of a reader,' Ben says. 'I read no fiction or no memoir type stuff at all.'

I stay quiet, and after a while Ben seems to consider something carefully, within himself, and then he says, 'Listen, as long as what you're writing is true, and is not being cruel, you must write what you like to express. It does not matter if that is about Dad, or about me, or about you. If you are being truthful, then it is good with me.'

I let that sit between us for a few seconds. Ben sits back and cocks his head slightly.

'Well, maybe I can give you some to read,' I say. 'I'm just not sure the stuff about Dad will be very good for you.'

He thinks about this, and remains noncommittal. 'Maybe one day I can read a bit. You can choose what you give me.'

We finish our meal. As we walk to our vehicles I tell Ben that we should not wait so long until we get together again.

He agrees, nods his head. 'For sure. But not next week, because we will not have anything to say to each other.'

I smile at this, at the evident, practical truth of it, and I ask Ben if sometime in about two months' time will suit him.

'Perfect,' he says.

We hug, and when I get into my car I see him walk towards the flower market.

RE: POIGNANCE

from: Paul <_____@gmail.com>
to: Ben <_____@gmail.com>
date: 22 October 2019, 18:41
subject: RE: Poignance
mailed-by: gmail.com
security: Standard encryption (TLS) <u>Learn more</u>

Dear Ben,

It was so good to see you yesterday. As promised, I'll try to be your memory, and I'll focus on poignance.

Let me just first say something about my memories.

I heard a great line on a podcast in my car, earlier today: *memories are like friends – they will betray you.*

I have little actual evidence for memories about my life; there are few who can corroborate. I have made and lost many friends, and there are none who have been around for the entire journey. I have contact with only two blood relatives: my mom, and (recently) you. There are two slim family photo albums. That is it.

This lack of evidence is by choice, and active design.

When I was a child, Dad (geographically removed) sent me letters, and for a while we also corresponded via audiotape. Every two weeks or so a new recording would arrive from him, I would listen and then record over this, telling him things about myself, then mail the tape back to him.

One of these tapes remains: on it, Dad tells me about his plans for my next visit, while he was studying psychology at UCT; on the other side of the tape I (then around eleven years old) tell him about school, and then I sing a song. There is one other recording of me as a very young child (maybe two or three years old), talking excitedly, then more singing.

Dad's letters were sent from Johannesburg, when he lived up there. Later on, the letters were from Cape Town, from when he was a mature, postgraduate student. And then there are letters that he wrote when he was in various mental health facilities.

After our Great Separation, in 1994, I wanted to erase him, render him void. And so I burnt all those letters. As I watched those flames, I remember thinking I would regret this, one day.

Eight or so years later I moved to England, to start a new job, and as I cleaned out my house, discarding old documents and other clutter, I hesitated when I held in my hands a plastic bag containing maybe sixty rolls of undeveloped film. This was from my youth, from the earliest years, all the way through Dad and my mom's marriages, up to when I expelled him from my life.

How odd, that my mom and I collected but never developed these rolls of film. Dad, my mom, and I took photographs, documenting all the time at a steady clip, a camera never far away, but the films remained in their unopened rolls. I burnt them too.

There are days when I regret destroying those letters, and those rolls of film. If I could choose now to have them available to me, I would elect to keep them. But the thing about empirics, about evidence, is that they overwhelm memory with their clinical accuracy. This renders memory fixed, rather than liberated. Just because something is demonstrably real it does not make it particularly true. Were our smiles real, in all of those photographs? Or were those images stills, like from a film set: facsimile, artifice rather than authentic? Is a painting, created from memory, not often more evocative, more truthful, than a photograph of the same event?

Yes, I do regret those fires, those little extinctions – but not entirely. In a way that destruction amplified my recall, which is mutable. The absence of empirical evidence means that I have had to work harder to remember, to process, to embellish, add, delete – not in order to deceive, but to capture truth rather than facts. A sort of poetry, I hope, more than journalism. Neurosis rendered useful, I think.

Having said that, here are a few poignant memories, in six paragraphs:

At age nine, they smuggle me into the drive-in outside Bloemfontein, to see *Robin and Marian*, with Audrey Hepburn and Sean Connery in a middle-aged iteration of the tale. In the last scene – Robin is dying – he asks Marian for his bow and an arrow and shoots it out the window. Bury me where it lands, he says. Dad tears up, breathes through his nose, and when he's calm, on the way home, he tells me about 'poignance', and how affecting he found the sound of that arrow, departing from that scene. *Whack*, he says, trying to make the sound. *Whack*. And he looks out the car window, away from us.

In Hillbrow, where I visit him at age eleven, Dad walks with me in the petrichor, thunder still abundant, in the early evening, on the way to a bookshop. We cross the road and his arm is slung casually around my shoulders. He gives a little snort, says, 'Isn't it funny how they look at us, that couple?' I turn around and see a man staring after us, scowling, shaking his head. 'He thinks I'm a dirty old man. Fuck 'em,' says Dad, 'I'll keep my son close if I want.' He kisses me on the top of my head as we walk.

A year later, he's moved to George, to teach English at a school in the coloured township. My mother drives me across the Outeniqua Mountains every second Friday after school, from Oudtshoorn, and for a weekend we do father–son things. Shiny russians and chips for dinner, videos on Saturday night. We cry together when Orca the Killer Whale loses his partner and the young calf. On these visits, upon arrival, I am allowed to go to a specific drawer in the kitchen and collect a two-strip KitKat, waiting for me.

When I'm fourteen, we are stuck in traffic, in Cape Town, on our way to see *Kiss of the Spider Woman*. I'm too young, but I'm tall for my age and we'll sneak in. Dad explains the use of sex, in cinema, talks to me about the use of the camera – the thrilling aperture – and of kitschiness in art, as described in Kundera. He explains the word 'analogy' to me, segueing into etymology. He tells me about Marxism, and uses worker exploitation in the Cape Winelands as an example. On the way he stops at a petrol station; when he comes back I can smell it on him.

When I'm eighteen the depression is bad, and for two months during my first year at university I move in with him, and with you and your mom. I take the train to university, from where you live near her surgery, close to the townships. I breathe in the cold morning air, the metal smell of the tracks, and then he's there, taps me on the shoulder. He suggests we have a secret day. We go for breakfast at the Springbok Café, we take a drive in the mountains, and we go back to a tree where we'd carved our initials, years before. We listen to Tammy Wynette on the tape deck in the car, and we laugh at the lyrics. 'Kitschiness in art,' he reminds me.

A month before The Event, and our great estrangement, we run together in the vineyards. It is very early in the morning and there is a mist. The dogs keep getting in front of us, but it doesn't bother him. He's telling me about the role of the feminine spirit, in messianic Judaism, and how this moderates the harshness of patriarchy in the monotheistic traditions. He chants a couplet of something, from Hebrew apparently, and when I look at him, while we run, he winks at me. I don't know if God exists, I tell him. Doesn't matter, he says, meaning it. You have to kill Him, anyway, he says.

There's more where that came from – I just need to remember it. I'll tell you more on the way to Sutherland, to look for Capella.

Take care, brother –

P.

THE SENSE OF AN ENDING

Amongst my brother's Facebook photographs, there is a recent image of the man he calls Dad.

The photographer himself is visible, if you know where to look. You can catch Ben and his camera, reflected in the window, more than half obscured. From this angle he looks like a phantom behind glass, behind the burglar bars.

There is a garish old couch. It occurs to me that there are very few domestic objects indeed more bereft – more sad – than a soft, ugly couch outside on a back stoep.

Something is going on in the yard: they appear to be building some kind of vegetable patch. I did not ask when I was shown this photograph. I made a point not to ask.

The old man is tending to a braai, or rather, to meat being cooked on what looks like a braai. He looks like a vagrant inspecting the contents of a rubbish bin. There is a hole in his coat, and a piece of string hangs from the one corner. His trousers are too short, but this may be because he is bending over.

The old man is wearing disposable glasses – the kind you can get at a pharmacy, for specific distances. He is wearing a beanie hat, so I am unable to see how much hair loss there has been over the years. (This interests me, genetically.)

He does not look healthy. I am told there is something wrong with his lungs.

I try to locate and name the emotion that I am feeling.

Not indifference. Not disgust.

Pity – yes, pity comes close.

But the couch is sadder.

ACKNOWLEDGEMENTS

The two section titles, 'Time past' and 'Time present', are from 'Burnt Norton', no. 1 of T. S. Eliot's *Four Quartets*.

The title and structure of the opening chapter, 'I remember,', are taken from *The Sense of an Ending* by Julian Barnes, published in 2011 by Random House.

Earlier sections and/or versions of the chapter 'Tones of glass' appeared in *Tydskrif vir Letterkunde* 37(3/4) (1999), *Klyntji* online (21 September 2018), and in *New Contrast* 47(187) (2019).

The line '. . . eyes gleaming like a child's as he witnesses a house on fire' in the chapter 'Tones of glass' is derived from the line '. . . oë blink soos 'n kind s'n tydens 'n ramp' in Pieter Paul Fourie's short story 'Minnaars en kadawers', which was published in *Tydskrif vir Letterkunde* 29(4) (November 1991).

An earlier version of the chapter 'The line of beauty' was published as 'Arvo Pärt, for a man apart' in the *Mail & Guardian* on 11 September 2015.

The summary of Oscar Wilde's story 'The Happy Prince', in the chapter of that title, is adapted from *Complete Works of Oscar Wilde*, published in 2003 by Collins Classics.

An earlier version of the chapter 'I preferred Martin' was published in *Ons Klyntji* (no. 123) in 2019.

The line 'I remembered the shining boy in the green jersey, so alive on his bicycle, hand aloft, shouting my name – 'Paul!' – and the brave, terrified smile' in the chapter 'I preferred Martin' is based on a description that was used in the British television series *House of Cards*, which itself is based on the eponymous novel by Michael Dobbs.

The penultimate paragraph in the chapter 'Sons and lovers' is inspired by a reflection towards the end of the movie *The Man Without a Face*, which itself is based on Isabelle Holland's 1972 novel of the same name.

The final reflection ('but not enough') in the chapter 'Counterfactual' is taken from the film *Torch Song Trilogy* (1988), which itself is based on Harvey Fierstein's plays.

An earlier version of the chapter 'The second coming out' was published in Robin Malan and Ashraf Johaardien's *Yes, I Am! Writing by South African Gay Men*, published in 2010 by Junkets.

The line 'think of the skins I'd have to shed' in the chapter 'Lost, found, remain' is taken from Liza Minnelli's song 'So Sorry, I Said'.

The line 'solid and serene as a mid-ocean wave' in the chapter 'Grey' is taken from Helen Macdonald's memoir *H Is for Hawk*, which was published in 2014 by Jonathan Cape.

A section of the description of Mendelssohn's Violin Concerto in E minor, in the chapter 'Grey', is taken from Simon Keefe's *The Cambridge Companion to the Concerto*, published in 2005 by Cambridge University Press.

ABOUT THE AUTHOR

P.P. FOURIE was born in the Free State, and went to school in Clarens, Bloemfontein, and Oudtshoorn. He currently lives in Wellington, and he teaches in the Department of Political Science at Stellenbosch University. His short fiction – in Afrikaans and English – has appeared in *Tydskrif vir Letterkunde, Scrutiny2, New Contrast, Ons Klyntji*, and on LitNet. His non-fiction book *The Political Management of HIV and AIDS in South Africa: One burden too many?* (Palgrave Macmillan) was long-listed for the Alan Paton Award in 2006.